## "You're going to need all your energy tonight..."

It was the way Ainsley said it that made Ben do a double take.

She smiled but didn't look at him. "Those abs really were impressive. I might like a little alone time with them."

"So are you saying you want to touch them?" He'd always been direct, and wasn't into games.

"Yep, all over."

He laughed. "Well, at least you're honest. What happened to not wanting to date?"

"I didn't say anything about a date. I just want to run my hands across those abs more than I want to breathe."

He nearly tripped.

"It's bad for me to want you this much," she said. "But those abs mixed with that big heart of yours is kind of my kryptonite. Just sayin'."

"Ainsley, my abs are waiting for you..."

Dear Reader,

The holidays can be a wonderful time for so many, and at the same time painful for those who are alone, or who have loved ones deployed overseas. I wanted this book to reflect happier times. So for my Marine, Ben, his first Christmas spent at home in a long while had to be one filled with love and surprises.

He and Ainsley represent the good in the universe to me. They are from different worlds, but they find their way to one another.

I'd love to hear from you on Twitter, @candacehavens, or on Facebook. I hope that you have a glorious holiday season filled with love and joy.

*Candace*

# Candace Havens

---

## Christmas with the Marine

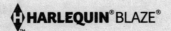

Recycling programs
for this product may
not exist in your area.

ISBN-13: 978-0-373-79919-0

Christmas with the Marine

Copyright © 2016 by Candace Havens

Printed in U.S.A.

www.Harlequin.com

**Candace "Candy" Havens** is a bestselling and award-winning author. She is a two-time RITA® Award, Write Touch Readers' Award and Holt Medallion finalist. She is also a winner of the Barbara Wilson Award. Candy is a nationally syndicated entertainment columnist for FYI Television. A veteran journalist, she has interviewed just about everyone in Hollywood. You can hear Candy weekly on New Country 96.3 KSCS in the Dallas–Fort Worth area.

### Books by Candace Havens

### Harlequin Blaze

*Take Me If You Dare*
*She Who Dares, Wins*
*Truth and Dare*
*Her Last Best Fling*

### *Uniformly Hot!*

*Model Marine*
*Mission: Seduction*
*Her Sexy Marine Valentine*
*Make Mine a Marine*

To get the inside scoop on Harlequin Blaze and its talented writers, visit Facebook.com/BlazeAuthors.

All backlist available in ebook format.

Visit the Author Profile page at Harlequin.com for more titles.

This book is dedicated to the Blaze readers.
Thank you for all of your support.

# 1

MARINE MAJOR BEN HAWTHORNE had served three tours in the Middle East. He'd survived being shot and a near-fatal helicopter crash. But this… This was beyond his capabilities. This is what happened when people gambled.

They ended up in giant toy stores in the Barbie aisle, trying to find the right one for a six-year-old orphan.

He'd rather go on another tour. Not that he didn't want the child to have her toy, it was just difficult. There were so many. Doctor ones and scientists, and an underwater one. And they came in all sizes. But all the child had listed was "Barbie." And Ben had lost a bet with his friends, so he was on his own buying more than one hundred gifts for the Toys for Tots program.

And he'd do it. As a kid, he'd lived through more than one Christmas without much under the tree. He understood how it felt to wake up with next to nothing there, not that it had bothered him much back then. He'd tried to make sure his little sister always had at least a couple of toys, even if they weren't exactly what she wanted. Seeing that smile of hers was something he'd sorely missed while being out of the country for the past ten years.

So he felt a lot of responsibility to get this right. That was one of the reasons he hadn't thrown much of a fit when he'd lost the bet.

Still, a Barbie was not his forte. GI Joe maybe, even Superman, but these dolls were beyond him.

"Hey, are you okay?" He glanced down to see a pair of light blue eyes staring back at him. They reminded him of the color of the sky on a clear day and were framed by a heart-shaped face and beautiful long strawberry-blond hair.

"What?"

*Well, that was cool. Beautiful woman talking. Pay attention.*

"You keep looking at the list and then the shelf. Do you need help? Are you buying something for your daughter?"

Her voice was soft and she didn't have a drawl like most of the people who lived in Corpus Christi. Even a lot of the guys on the base where he taught had a Texas accent. He'd grown used to it.

"Do you work here?" Of course she didn't work here. She was dressed in an expensive leather jacket and jeans and carrying one of those purses that probably cost more than his truck. The last woman he'd dated had treated that same kind of purse like it was her child. She'd definitely liked the purse more than she had him.

This lady laughed and heat warmed his lower regions. *Come on*, he told himself, *she's trying to help you*.

"No, but thanks to my twin nieces I'm well versed in everything Barbie. If you tell me a bit more about the little girl, I can probably help you."

She was beautiful, but more than that, he was desperate. If she could just point him in the right direction, he'd be her love slave for life.

Where the heck did that come from? *Dude, chill*.

He handed her the list. "It says she wants to be a vet when she grows up," he said. "Each kid has a short, one-line description about them."

Her eyebrow went up as she scanned the page. He pointed to the name of Jolie, the little girl in question. "She also likes puppies."

"This is a long list of kids. Your family must be huge." She frowned as her chin dropped and then she flipped to the next page and then the next. "There's more than fifty names here."

"Oh, no." He laughed. "I kind of lost a bet and I'm having to get the gifts for the Toys for Tots program. I'm from the Marine base." He pulled the other list out of his back pocket. "I also have a list of elderly patients from a nursing home facility who also need gifts." It was the last time he'd be playing poker with his friends Brody and Matt. They'd been in charge of the Christmas event, and now it was all on him.

"Wow. That must have been some bet."

He grunted. "Yep. Anyway, we have a fund everyone on the base donates to throughout the year, and then the first week of December we try to buy as many items as the money allows."

"This, my friend, is your lucky day." She grinned again, and then actually winked one of those beautiful blue eyes. It did all kinds of crazy things to his body.

Funny, he was thinking the same thing—about it being his lucky day. He'd practically been sent an angel for his very own Christmas present. He cleared his throat. "How's that?"

"Well, I happen to be a professional shopper."

His brows drew together. "So you like to shop?"

"More than that, it's my business. I shop for busy professionals. That's why I'm here. On the hunt for a few gifts for a CEO's kids."

"Wait. People pay you to shop for them?"

She smirked. "Yes. It's a *real* profession, and I do just fine, thank you."

He'd offended her, and held up his hands in surrender. "Sorry. I've just never heard of anything like that. But it's cool. I didn't mean to insult you. I'm the guy standing here staring at a million dolls without a clue what to do."

She shrugged. "I'm used to the attitude. My family feels that way about my chosen profession. Since you're doing this for charity, and I think it's sweet you're taking this so seriously, trying to find the right gift for each child, I'll help for free."

"Oh, I don't mind paying for your services." That sounded really wrong. A woman walked past them and gave them a dirty look. "I mean, uh, I'd be grateful. So much so that I'll pay the fee."

She started laughing. "Sweet. But you can't afford me."

Another woman walked by, yanking her kids along, giving them more dirty looks. They would get arrested if they kept this up.

"Before we get thrown out, maybe I should hurry up and say thanks. And can I buy you dinner, at least?"

She laughed nervously. "Hmm. We'll see." She held out her hand. "I'm Ainsley Garrett."

He shook her hand and her skin was so smooth. "I'm Ben Hawthorne, and thanks again."

"Go get two more carts. I'll start on your list."

Two hours and six carts of toys later, he had everything he was supposed to buy. He and one of the store clerks were piling the bags in the back of his SUV when Ainsley walked out carrying a couple of large bags of her own.

"Hey," he called to her and waved. "I really would like to thank you. Let me take you to dinner."

"It isn't necessary. Besides, I have plans." And just like that she shot him down. Figured. Someone as beautiful as she was wouldn't be alone. But at least he'd tried.

"Okay, but I feel guilty about not paying you for your time."

"No worries. It was fun."

If she said so. Even though the toys were for a good cause, shopping gave him a headache.

She turned and walked away, and he wanted to say something. Pull her back into his orbit. Even though he understood she was way out of his league—from her designer shoes to those sunglasses perched on top of her head—he was sad their time together was up.

*Pathetic.* Yeah, but it had been a long time since he'd met a woman like her. Maybe never. He hadn't seen a ring, but she might have a boyfriend or be engaged, and he didn't poach.

He'd seen too many of his fellow Marines cheated on by lonely spouses left back home. So he was wary of that sort of thing. And it was one of many reasons he wasn't big on long-term anything. He was married to his job and planned to stay that way for the foreseeable future.

He turned to finish helping the clerk with the last of the bags.

"Hey," she said.

He glanced back.

"So, do you have to wrap all those gifts by yourself?"

Shoot. He hadn't even thought of that. He pinched the bridge of his nose. "Man, that didn't even occur to me." It was the truth. He'd have to buy paper, and he was the world's worst gift-wrapper, not that he'd done it that often. A few times, he'd sent things home while he was overseas, but he never wrapped them.

"Give me your phone."

Was she giving him her phone number? Things were looking up.

She typed into his phone and then handed it back to him. It was an address.

Even better.

"Tomorrow, meet me there at twelve forty-five. The drill team is holding their annual craft fair."

"Drill team?" What was she talking about?

"They have a gift-wrapping service. For a dollar donation per gift they'll wrap it and do a beautiful job."

"Thank you. I'll definitely do that. Wait? Did you say meet you there?"

She nodded. "Yes. Give me your list for the nursing home."

He pulled the paper out of his back pocket. She perused it again.

"What's your budget?"

"We have eleven hundred dollars, but I was going to add a little more if we needed it."

"I think that should be plenty. I'll pick these gifts up for you and meet you at the high school tomorrow. See ya."

"Hold on. Don't you need money for the gifts?"

"Not yet. You can give it to me tomorrow. How gullible are you giving your money to a stranger?"

"You just helped me buy a couple thousand dollars' worth of toys for children. I'm pretty sure I can trust you." She didn't bother to turn around.

What kind of person went and bought all those gifts without taking the cash?

Look on the bright side, he told himself, at least you'll see her the next day. That idea for the gift wrapping was awesome. The whirlwind that was Ainsley had saved him. Again.

"Thanks," he said belatedly. But it was to air. He hadn't even seen where she'd gone.

*Hmm.* She was so beautiful and kind. Hard combination to find sometimes.

But so out of his league.

Yes, she was. And he had a feeling she was going to fuel a whole lot of fantasies for a while.

*Yep. Enjoy your dreams.* Since that was about the only way a guy like him was going to get a woman like her.

AS HARD AS SHE tried not to, Ainsley stole a look in her rearview mirror at Ben. That man was too gorgeous for words with his muscles, chiseled jaw and close-cut Marine haircut. Her mouth had gone dry when she'd seen the big muscled man in a uniform searching for dolls, of all things. He'd been so serious, trying to find the right gifts for kids, as if he was on the mission of a lifetime. He'd been so enthusiastic about making sure those children had a great Christmas that it had been contagious. It had been the most fun she'd had in a really long time.

He had a heart.

It was something she was pretty sure had been missing from the last three guys she'd dated, two of whom her parents had picked out for her. She'd never trust them again. The men they pointed out to her were all narcissistic jerks, every one of them. And she couldn't imagine any of them, losing a bet or not, shopping for gifts for a bunch of kids and the elderly.

That tugged at her in a way she couldn't ignore.

*No. No more men. The next two years I'll be focused on growing my business.*

Ben lifted his arms to close the back of his SUV and his shirt pulled loose from his jeans. Those abs.

*Chiseled* was the only word that came to mind. Like they'd been carved in stone.

She sucked in a breath.

*Oh, my.* She fanned herself and waited for him to pull out of the parking lot before backing out her hybrid. That was a M-A-N.

Though it had been work she'd had a good time today. She and Ben had laughed as they questioned some of the toys' characteristics. Like a doll that pooped, and one that had the creepiest voice as it called for its mama. It made them both shiver, and then chuckle out loud.

After they'd picked up the gifts for the girls on the list, they'd been to the aisle with all the Matchbox cars.

"I bet you had a ton of these when you were a kid," she'd said.

He'd held one of the sports cars with reverence. "No..." His voice had been a whisper and then he'd frowned. And that's when she'd noticed he didn't have a lot of experience with toys...at all. Everything seemed new to him.

What kind of childhood had he had?

It made her feel selfish because she'd never wanted for anything. Ever. She'd wanted to ask him about his past, but it didn't seem right. And she had the sense that it might make him sad. They only had a few hours together and she hadn't wanted to ruin it.

It also felt good to help someone in need. Okay, she did that every day. Her job gave her the greatest joy, as she helped her clients find the perfect gifts for their loved ones, employees and friends. But making kids and old people happy—that was a different level of giving.

Her phone rang. "Accept call," she said.

"Hello?" Bebe said. Her trusty partner's British accent came through loud and clear. Ainsley wasn't sure what she'd do without her best friend—the woman was a master scheduler and kept their finances in order. She also wasn't afraid to talk to a client about a bill, which was something that made Ainsley really uncomfortable. Talking about money always did. Bebe had started as an assistant, but had quickly become her partner in crime.

"Are you there?"

"I'm here," she said as she left the parking lot, her mind still on the Marine. "And, yes, I know I'm running late. I got caught up doing some charity work. I'll drop Bob's presents off for you to wrap, and then I'll head out to Clinical South." The head administrator wanted to discuss gifts for the staff, and for any of the patients who would be stuck in the facility over the holidays.

This really was their busiest time of year and she'd spent too much of her packed schedule helping the hot guy.

"That's why I'm calling. They actually pushed you to tomorrow. I've been trying to call for the last hour. Did you leave your phone in the car again?"

No. She'd been distracted by the glorious man in uniform.

"I didn't hear it ring."

"I swear I'm going to put 'The Imperial March' on

your phone so you hear when I call. Anyway, Craig Price at CIM wants to meet with you about gifts for his staff. He had a four o'clock open. Can I tell them you'll be there?"

She sighed. Craig was an ex. One of the several narcissists she'd dated, though he hadn't been as bad as some of the others. He was married to his job, though, and when he thought it was okay to go six months between calling for dates, they parted ways. But his technology company, CIM, had over four hundred employees—that was a pretty tidy commission for her company.

But Craig. *Ugh.*

"I know he's a prat, but that commission pays the mortgage for a year. I'd go, but I'm meeting with the Funky Monkey folks at three. They have a bunch of new merchandise they're bringing by."

"I wish we could switch," she said. She loved the boutique called Funky Monkey more than just about any other. The owner, Amy, was one of the most creative people she'd ever met.

"I promise to nab something shiny for you. Craig specifically asked for you. Maybe he wants to apologize for being such a fool. And hello, we promised ourselves a Christmas bonus this year if we made our goals, and we're so very close."

She had a point. And this was business. In the two years she'd been operating, she'd had to handle much worse. Some of her wealthiest clients, a few of whom were her parents' friends, felt entitled and had to be treated that way. Even after she'd grown up around that sort of wealth, their attitudes chewed at her gut. But she wasn't dumb. The client was always right. Even if they were jerks sometimes. Well, as long as they paid their bills.

"Yep. You're right. Yes, I can do four. Do you have suggestions? Did they give you a budget?"

"Yes, on both counts. His assistant gave me the run-down on what type of gifts and how much they wanted to spend for each level from the board on down."

Ainsley did love it when they were organized. "Okay, good. That makes our job easier. Can you print out the ideas and put a book together for me?"

They did most of their presentations on a laptop or tablet, but clients liked to have something they could hold in their hands and peruse. It was a trick she'd learned early on. Folks tended to buy more when they could feel the pages. Weird, but true.

"Already working on it."

"And that, my friend, is why I love you best."

"Yes, luv, remember that when it's time for my raise." Ainsley smiled. Bebe could give herself a raise whenever she wanted, although they would discuss it first, as they did everything.

"Yes, ma'am. Okay, so I'll see you in a bit."

That's what she needed—a reminder of what was most important. Her work. This was their most important time of the year. The last thing she wanted to deal with was a distraction.

Especially a hot Marine.

She took another deep breath.

A very hot, sexy Marine.

# 2

THE HIGH SCHOOL cafeteria buzzed with activity. And it was loud. Really loud. Ben wasn't a huge fan of big crowds or noise, but this was for a good cause. There were booths with everything from wooden toys to homemade candles to miniature Christmas trees. He'd never seen anything like it.

"Explain to me again why we're here and not watching the game? It's almost the end of football season," Matt complained.

"I bought the toys, you guys have to help me haul them in to get them wrapped." It would have taken him thirty trips from the car and back without his friends.

He searched the throng of people for the pretty blonde, but he didn't see her. Dang if he hadn't thought about her all night.

Jake grinned and tightened his grip on the bags he was carrying. It was as if his buddy could read his thoughts.

Mari, Brody's wife and mother of his child, bustled up next to him.

"I think it's sweet that you're doing this," Mari said to Ben. "You're helping the Toys for Tots program *and* the fund-raiser for the drill team. You're my hero."

Brody cleared his throat. "I thought I was your hero."

"Oh, honey, always. Always." She kissed him, and Ben had to look away. Sometimes their intimacy bothered him. He wasn't sure why. Maybe because he'd never been that close to another person. He'd dated a lot of women, but none that made him feel the way that Brody talked about his wife. And his friend Matt was a goner, as well, with his fiancée, Chelly. His buddies were so wrapped up in their women, and Ben just didn't get it.

He was attracted to the women he dated, but his interest waned after a short while. The guys on the base where he taught helicopter maintenance classes, tested the machines and helped out with training missions called him Casanova because he had a different girl every week.

There was one woman he definitely wanted to spend time with, but he had a feeling she was far beyond his reach.

It took a few minutes but they finally found the booth set up for gift wrapping. It was staffed by a bunch of young girls, with ponytails, in stretch pants and T-shirts that read Dance with Me.

"You want us to wrap how many?" one of the young girls asked. She had her hair piled so high on her head it almost added another foot.

She gave him a once-over, and it was all he could do not to laugh. Where was Ainsley?

"Yes, and I'll donate two dollars a package, which is a dollar more than you guys usually ask for," Ben said. Even at this young age, money talked.

The girl's smile grew, and then a woman came up behind her. She held out her hand. "Hi, I'm Coach Kaylie. That's very generous of you. May I ask who these toys are for? There are a lot of them." She didn't look much older than the girl giving him a tough time.

"Toys for Tots," Jake said, as he patted Ben on the back. "Our boy here picked them all out, but we need help wrapping them."

"Terrific," Kaylie said. "That's so kind that you're doing this for kids. Of course we'll help you. And we really appreciate the donation. We're trying to get to three different dance competitions this year, so every penny counts." She batted her eyelashes at Jake.

This time Ben did chuckle. Jake had that effect on women. Never failed.

"Wonderful," a woman's voice said. He glanced down to see Ainsley. She was here, and she looked every bit as beautiful as she had the day before. He'd been sure his imagination had been playing tricks on him.

Today, she wore jeans and boots that came up to her knees. But it was the tight white sweater that nearly did him in. Her body was the stuff of fantasies. His fantasies.

Once again he found himself clearing his throat, and he positioned the bag he was carrying so no one would see the sudden tent in his pants.

*Crap.* Sad puppies. Old, crinkly people. He had to think of something that was not the beautiful woman beside him.

"Hi," he said. *Well, that was brilliant.*

She beamed up at him. "I've brought the rest of your gifts. Got them first thing this morning. Since they're for the nursing home, I asked the girls to put them in bags with tissue so it would be easier for those arthritic hands to open," she said sweetly. "They should be just about finished with those."

"You really do think of everything."

"Part of the job."

"Oh," Kaylie said. "This is the guy you were talking about?"

"Yes," Ainsley, said waving a hand to the group of kids wrapping at the tables behind the coach. There was now a bunch of boys, as well. "I'm glad you picked up some more volunteers."

"Yeah, I never seem to have a hard time getting the football and basketball teams to help out the dancers. Though, keeping a constant eye on them isn't always the easiest." Kaylie laughed. "We should be done in about thirty minutes with the seniors' gifts, and we'll need a few hours for the tots."

Brody groaned behind him.

"It's okay, guys, if you want to go on home." He turned back to Kaylie. "Can some of those players help me load the truck later?"

"Absolutely," she said.

"I'll stay," Jake offered. "I don't mind volunteering

if you need help," he said to Kaylie. "I'm not much good at wrapping, but I'm good at other things."

Kaylie and Ainsley both roared with laughter.

"What?" Jake asked innocently. "I meant I can keep an eye on the players to make sure they aren't trying to put the moves on these lovely young ladies."

The dancers giggled and whispered to one another.

"I might take you up on that," Kaylie said. "You two," she called out, pointing to Ainsley and Ben, "go look around and come back in a couple of hours. We'll have everything ready."

"That sounds like a good plan," Brody said. "I'm going to search for Mari. Make sure she doesn't need help with anything. Matt, I can give you a ride back."

They waved goodbye and then left.

Ainsley crooked her arm through his. "Come on, Marine. I'll buy you lunch and we can check out the booths. I have a few homemade gifts on my list. I might find them here."

He'd walk across hot coals to spend a little time with her, so he could easily handle the loud noise of the craft fair a little longer. "Only if you let me buy," he said.

"Sure. If you really want to."

"Hey, you've donated a lot of time and like I said, I owe you a meal at the very least."

"Whatever. Come on."

He thought they'd head back to the parking lot. He planned on taking her somewhere nice. Instead, she pulled him through a maze of booths to reach the other end of the cafeteria.

"Hold up, you want to eat here?"

"Yes," she said. "This booth has the best chili pies."

She walked up to the window. "Who made the chili today?" she asked the elderly woman manning the cash box.

"Frank," the woman replied. "He doesn't let anyone else touch it. Doesn't want to ruin his reputation. What can I get for you?"

"You are in for a treat," Ainsley said to Ben. "Frank is an award-winning chili star. His daughter, Amber, is on the drill team. He's pretty much the best thing about coming to the craft fair."

She turned to the woman. "We need two chili pies and a Coke. And what do you want to drink?" she said to him.

"Water is good." He didn't drink a lot of soda. He tried to avoid sugar and he was careful about what he ate, too. Not that he had a lot of choice when he was deployed. You ate what the mess hall gave you or what was in your pack. But when he was stateside he ate fresh food whenever he could. He'd learned to cook when he was kid. It'd helped out his mom because she had to work so much of the time.

"You okay?" Ainsley was handing him a bottle of water.

"What? Yeah. Sorry. I've never had a chili pie."

"No way. Fritos and chili and cheese. Best things ever. Are you some kind of health nut? Is that how you have that hot bod?" Her eyes flashed as if she'd realized what she'd just said.

"You think I'm hot?"

"Marine, everyone here thinks you're hot."

A grin spread across his face. "Uh, thanks. But I don't think everyone's looking at me, I have a feeling all eyes are on you. How could they not be? You're gorgeous."

She snorted. "You're so polite."

"You don't know how beautiful you are, do you?"

She shrugged. "Don't really think about it. Let's go sit. Can't believe I'm hanging out with a chili pie virgin. This is going to be fun."

He nearly tripped when she said the word *virgin*. He picked up their drinks, so she could grab the cardboard containers with their food. The chili didn't smell too bad, and he was hungry. She led him to an orange table with matching plastic chairs. Been a long time since he'd eaten in a high school cafeteria.

"Make sure you get some Fritos in that first bite. It's the salty mixed with the chili spices that makes it worthy of worship."

He did what she'd told him and it was…good. Really good. "I had no idea corn chips could taste like this."

"I know, right? So amazing." She took a swig of her drink. "How long have you been in the Marines?"

"Joined up the week I graduated from high school. Best way I could think of to take care of my mom and little sister. It was decent pay, and I didn't have to worry about living expenses so I could send them just about everything I made."

She blinked and he wasn't sure if those were tears in her eyes.

"Did I say something to upset you?"

"No. Not at all. You risked your life when you were nothing but a kid to take care of your family?"

"Yeah. And I'll admit, it seemed cool at the time. Fighting for my country. But I had no idea what I was getting into. Still, I wouldn't trade being a Marine for anything."

She blinked again.

"Are you okay?" he asked.

"Yep. I've just never met a selfless man before. You're an anomaly."

Her compliment made him laugh.

"I don't know about that. Maybe you just haven't met the right guys."

"True that." She wiped some chili from the corner of her mouth with a paper napkin. "I'm so impressed that even that young you were looking after your people. Wow, when I was eighteen, I was an idiot. Partying in college and making bad choices." She rolled her eyes. "Really bad choices."

He chuckled. "Well, if I'd had the opportunity, I probably would have made worse choices, another reason why my mom didn't fuss too much when I went off to boot camp. She knew I needed the discipline. I was never a bad kid, but I didn't always make the smart choices, especially in high school. My grades were low." Of course, a lot of that had to do with being tired from working sometimes as many as two jobs after school. There wasn't anything he wouldn't do to help his family.

It had taken his mom challenging the principal in

front of the school board before they finally gave him some grace. His mom was a lot of great things, and fierce was one of them. Never in his life had he won an argument with her, and the principal had learned that the hard way.

"Still," she said, "it took me another four years before I figured out what I wanted to do. And another year after that before I finally had the guts to do it. What you do is heroic and dangerous. It takes a special type of person to do that job. To run toward the scary when everyone else is running away."

"We don't really think about it that way." He wanted to find out more about her, and he'd never been comfortable talking about himself. "I'm curious how you make money shopping for people."

She blanched.

Shoot. He'd done it again. "No, no. I mean, I think it's a cool job. And I'm curious about how it works. Oh, and that reminds me." He pulled out a wad of cash. "How much do I owe you?"

"You can pay me later. I have receipts for you in my car. I was able to get some of the stuff donated when I told them what it was for, so I bought twice as much. I hope that's okay. Maybe these elderly people might enjoy getting more than one gift. It's small stuff, mostly, to make their lives more comfortable. Only spent a little over half your budget and that's with the wrapping. I'll have to look at the receipts but it was right around six hundred."

"You are good at this. We can donate the rest to

the charity. Are you sure I can't compensate you in some way?"

She shook her head. "Nope. And to answer your question, I usually get a commission. A negotiated percentage of the whole budget. A lot of what I do is for corporate clients. Finding the perfect gifts for their staff or for guests they have coming in, or finding giveaways for trade shows. We have a whole division for that last thing, and by division, I mean that's mostly what my partner, Bebe, handles, where she finds promotional swag for different companies."

He swallowed the last bit of chili. "That's interesting. I didn't even know a business like that existed."

She put down her fork. "Yeah, my grandmother actually helped me figure it out."

"Did she have the same kind of business?"

"Oh, no. She's a retired professor who lives in Ireland now. But she's always had a knack for finding the perfect gifts for people. Like an intuitiveness for knowing what's wanted. I sort of inherited it from her. I know that sounds weird, but I get this gut feeling for what's right for folks. And after college, I wasn't quite sure what to do with that awesome philosophy degree I had."

"Wow. I didn't see that one coming," he said honestly. He figured an MBA or something.

"What? I can spout Plato and Charles Hartshorne with the best of them."

"I know the first, never heard of the second."

"Trust me, most people haven't. But about two months after I graduated, I was working as a personal shopper at Neiman Marcus in Dallas. I really wasn't qualified to do anything else. I was promoted three times in six months. Grandma said I should take what I was best at and apply it to my career goals. 'But never work for the man.' Did I mention Grandma is a bit of a hippie, much to the chagrin of my mom, her daughter?

"Anyhoo, I took some business classes and decided to open my own personal-shopping service. There are a lot of them in Dallas and the competition is stiff. But there wasn't here in Corpus, so I came home and... Wow, I'm telling you my life story." She rolled her eyes.

"Nah, I'm intrigued. And your grandma sounds supersmart and practical."

"She's brilliant. Taught at Oxford. Still lives over there. She's my favorite philosopher."

"Ah, and it comes full circle. Oxford? Wow. That's pretty fancy." All this info made him even more curious about Ainsley. She was intelligent and beautiful, a dangerous combination. He could sit here all afternoon listening to her talk.

That had never happened before.

She nodded. "So I guess you didn't mind the chili pie, after all?"

He held up the empty container. "One of the best things I've eaten in a while. Who is this Frank guy?"

"He owns a barbeque place out by the beach, Duley's, which is named after his dad. They've been around a long time. And his ribs are even better than his chili."

"Maybe I could take you there some time?"

"I don't know. We'll see."

"You keep saying that. Do you have a thing about not dating guys in the military or something?"

Her head popped up. "A thing? No. Should I? And who says I want to date you?"

She had him there. He sounded like a jerk. "Sorry, I—"

She reached out and touched his arm. "I'm messing with you. Your face. That was classic. But I'm going to be straight with you. I'm focused on my career. I'm really not looking to date anyone right now. I don't have a lot of luck with guys, and I find them kind of self-centered. Not that you would be. But…if you want someone to hang out with today, I'm your girl. Want to come shopping with me?"

"Uh, sure?"

The way she talked—so fast—it took him a minute to catch up.

"And for the record," he said, clearing his throat, "I'm not looking to date, either. I simply wanted to thank you for helping me."

She chewed on her lip as she eyed him. "Okay. So," she began and waved to the empty containers, "we've had our meal. We should be good. You still want to hang out?"

He shrugged. With this one, it was probably best to play it cool. She didn't want to date. Well, he'd been honest when he said that wasn't his thing. His teaching at the base was keeping him busy, and besides, he didn't do relationships.

But he definitely wanted to spend more time with her. "I'm yours for the afternoon," he told her.

And a small voice inside said "and more," if she wanted.

# 3

BEN WAS SNIFFING some homemade candles at a booth, and Ainsley could not keep from staring at him. She had to stop ogling poor Ben, or he was going to get the wrong idea. But everything about him... Heck, she'd never been so attracted to a man. Never in her life had she believed in pheromones but it had to be something like that.

That and he had one of the most jaw-dropping examples of the male body she'd ever seen. Oh, and the fact he was sweet. Taking care of his mom and sister. Putting his life on the line for them, and his country.

A heart-stopping combo if ever there was one.

*How many times do I have to tell myself no more men?*

He glanced back and shot her one of his devastating smiles.

*At least a hundred.*

"My mom might like this vanilla one. Do you think giving her something like this would be a good Christmas gift?"

She nodded and smiled. "Everyone loves candles," she said.

"What else is on your list?" he asked her.

*Right. Stay on task.*

"I have gifts for two executives I need to pick up. The client wanted something homemade but nice. Classy. Wood sculptures or pens. There's a man here who crafts things out of old bourbon barrels. I usually buy him out. Those are popular gifts for men and women."

Her phone played Ozzie Osbourne's "Crazy Train." It was the ringtone for her sister, Megan.

"Just a second," Ainsley said.

"Help!" Megan yelled before Ainsley could even say hello.

"Megan, breathe." Her sister was a bit of a drama queen in all things, but she loved her. She was the only person who made worse choices when it came to men than Ainsley did.

"Sorry. I'm freaking out. The bachelor auction is tonight, and," she gasped and sniffled, "two of our guys had to cancel because they have the flu. I swear, if they're faking I will kill them both. Dead."

Ainsley thought to downplay the situation and scoffed, "It's fine, Megan. So you have a couple less bachelors. No biggie."

"Yes, biggie. It's for charity. I promised twenty of the hottest guys in Corpus. What am I doing to do with eighteen? And those guys were my big tickets, the two that backed out. My end-of-show wow factors."

"What?" Sometimes Megan talked in riddles.

"My moneymakers. They were going to push us over the top. I so wanted to beat Stephanie at her own game. She's been talking behind my back about how she was so much more organized last year. And it's true. But still. I want to win. And by win, I mean I want the children's cancer fund to make a ton of money. The most money ever."

Ainsley smiled. "You want to stick it to Stephanie in the worst way. Be honest."

"Yes. Okay. Fine. But the only way to do that is to get the most donations for these guys, right? So, it's a win-win, if I can make it happen. But I can't do that without some hot studly studs."

Her sister always had a way with words. "So call your friends. You know hundreds of guys." Megan went through men faster than she did shoes, and she really loved shoes.

Her sister sighed. "Yeah, unfortunately, I do. I've called in all the favors I could. A lot of my friends already donated the silent auction prizes. They don't like the idea of being in front of a bunch of drunk women trying to buy them."

"I can't imagine why." Ainsley had never liked these types of events for that reason. Even though the guys were doing it out of the goodness of their hearts, she always felt it was kind of humiliating. The whole objectifying them, and then there was the women pawing after them on the dance floor. No, she couldn't imagine why.

"Please," Megan begged. "You know everyone. Surely you can scrounge up a couple of super good-looking guys. I'll owe. Like, my life. Please don't make me beg more."

Ainsley glanced up to find Ben watching her intently. No. She couldn't. He wouldn't. But if ever there was a big moneymaker, it was him.

"Hold on." She put her phone on mute and gave him her best smile.

"What are you and Jake doing tonight?"

"I'D RATHER BE in the middle of a war zone with insurgents ready to take me down," Jake said, messing with his tie for the fiftieth time. Ben and Jake were both dressed in penguin suits for the charity auction. This was the worst idea in the history of ideas. That's what he got for giving in to a pretty face.

"Right there with you, brother."

When Ainsley had smiled that big, hopeful smile at him, he couldn't say no. Heck, he'd probably have done just about anything to spend time with her.

But this. Well, it was definitely beyond the call of duty. Ainsley had talked about kids with cancer, and that was all it took. He couldn't say no. And he'd coerced Jake into doing it with him by telling him not just about the charity, but that there would be hot women who wanted his body.

Jake seemed a lot more comfortable with that idea than Ben. He liked things quiet, without so many people. This would be mayhem. The sound of voices was growing louder and louder. The night had begun with free champagne and light appetizers since, as Megan had explained, "We like the women to be slightly tipsy because they spend more."

Ben didn't think that was a nice way to do things, but it was for the kids, which was what he kept telling himself. They'd just finished the video showing why the research needed to be done. There were some sniffles on the other side of the curtains.

"Sorry, ladies. That video gets me every time," the announcer said. "But now, let's turn up the music and have some fun." The announcer went on to explain how the women could bid.

His gut twisted. One by one the guys went and strutted their stuff. The screams grew louder every time. When the bidding began for the first guy, Ben never wanted to retreat more than he did right then.

"We're Marines. We can do this," Ben said, more to convince himself than anything.

Jake turned to face him.

"Oorah," they said together and high-fived. The other remaining bachelors laughed and shook their heads. They were pretty nice guys—had to be to do something like this.

"I bet I pull in twice as much as you," Jake said. This is what they did—challenged each other. They'd been on two tours together and humor was the one way they all dealt with the horror.

Ben grunted. "Only if they like their side of beef with a hunk of cheese," he said. "This," Ben said as he patted his abs, "is the real deal."

They both grinned. It was bravado, nothing more.

There was one more to go before it would be Jake's

turn. And then Ben was last. Ainsley had told him it was a prime spot, but man, he was feeling the pressure. Each bachelor was pulling in more than the next. The last guy had made two thousand for the charity.

The noise went up a couple of decibels and he and Jake peeked around the curtain. They were in a large hotel ballroom that had been set up for the event, with lots of tables and chairs, and a stage, or rather…a runway. It was a fancy affair with crystal chandeliers, gilt centerpieces and lots of pink and white flowers. Everyone was dressed up. None of the women were as beautiful as Ainsley, who wore a white gown that fit her curves. Her hair was up and she looked like a royal princess or an A-list movie star.

Damn, he couldn't' stop looking at her. She wasn't even paying attention to the guys, but was glancing down at her phone. And then, as if she sensed him, she met his eyes and gave him a little smile. And she winked. He loved it when she did that. Like they were in on their own little secret.

"So out of your league," Jake said when he figured out where Ben had been watching. Ainsley was sitting at a table, dead center.

"Yep," Ben said. The music volume went up a bit more, as did the screams. The noise was getting to him. This happened sometimes. He backed away from the curtain and bent over to put his hands on his thighs, drawing in deep breaths. He concentrated on his breathing like his therapist had taught him.

"Hey." Jake patted his shoulder. "It's just a bunch of crazy tipsy women. I was kidding. It's going to be okay.

It really isn't much different than the country bar we were at a few weeks ago. Remember all those women when we joined their line dance? At least, maybe these women won't puke beer on your shoes."

There was that. He'd had to toss out his favorite pair of cowboy boots because there was no coming back from that.

Ben hated this weakness. Nothing had ever bothered him until that last tour. They'd spent twenty-four hours holed up in a camp where they were hit with mortar after mortar. He'd been working maintenance on a downed Black Hawk. And they were only getting out when the chopper was fixed. Problem was, he didn't have the parts he needed. It took every mechanical brain cell he had to figure out how to create something makeshift to get them to safety.

And it wasn't as if he hadn't done that sort of thing hundreds of times. They were always in some hot zone. Always under pressure. But that one hit him. It was the noise. The constant *boom boom boom* of the electronic music.

"Oh, no," Jake said.

"What?" Ben glanced up to find his friend loosening up and cracking his neck like he was getting ready to go into the ring with a prizefighter.

"You're on," Megan said to Jake. Ainsley's sister was the reason they were there. She'd needed help, and Ainsley had turned to him. And with that smile.

"Good luck, dude," Ben said as he straightened and then high-fived his friend. "You got this."

The noise level rose even louder. Ben pushed it

away, focused on his breathing. He wouldn't disappoint Ainsley or her sister. All he had to do was walk to the end of the stage, stand there and wait for someone to say "sold," and he was done.

"Five thousand!" he heard a woman shout.

What the...? A date with Jake brought in five thousand dollars?

Ben had been hoping for maybe five hundred for himself. He'd even offered to give Ainsley two hundred and fifty if the bids didn't go up for him. She'd kept telling him that he had nothing to worry about, but there was no way he would bring in that kind of big money.

Ben popped his jaw. This was nuts. He was a confident guy. He'd never had problems with being appealing to women, and this was for charity. He was going to have fun.

*Sure. Keep telling yourself that, buddy.*

"Okay, ladies, we've got another treat for you," the announcer said. "Ben is a Marine, working on the base here in our lovely hometown. We hear he's great with his hands, and that his abs—well, are to *d-i-e* for. Ladies, let's welcome Ben."

The women cheered.

Ben laughed. Yep. He could do this. Raise the most money for those kids. He wouldn't be outdone by Jake. He didn't care if he had to strip to do it.

In fact... He quickly undid his shirt buttons and held his tie in his hand. When the curtain opened he tossed the bow tie out to the audience.

The screeching reached an all-time high, but he

forced a smile and walked to the end of the stage. His eyes found Ainsley, and his smile widened.

More screeching, but he wasn't really listening anymore. She was smiling back, and then she winked at him and mouthed something. He had no idea what she'd said, but he nodded as if he did.

Then she made a motion to pull his shirt open a little and to turn around in a circle. She was doing a twirly thing with her fingers.

*It's for charity.* He kept repeating the mantra to himself.

"Oh, my, we did not disappoint. Look at those abs, ladies. Those are scrumptious! And that tattoo. Does anyone have a fan? Now, can I get—" The announcer was interrupted.

"Two thousand," a woman shouted. Ben ripped his eyes away from Ainsley and gave the woman a little wave.

Whew. At least he wouldn't be some loser who didn't bring in any cash.

"Thirty-five hundred," another woman said.

All right, then. Things were looking up. Ben shook his head and laughed, then gave that lady an even bigger wave.

And so it went on. A few seconds later they were up to six thousand.

"Everyone wants to take home a Marine. We hear they never let a woman down."

"Ten thousand dollars," a woman at Ainsley's table shouted, as she stood up and waved her paddle. She was probably in her late thirties.

There was a huge gasp. Then clapping.

Ben wasn't sure he heard her right.

"That's ten thousand going once, twice and sold! That's table one, paddle thirty-five. And that's it, ladies. The table monitors will be by to take your checks and credit cards. Please don't forget to visit our silent auction next door. If you didn't get some time with your favorite bachelor, bid on that trip to Fiji. A tropical vacation will get your mind off your troubles. And those raffle tickets for the Audi are still available. That thing is definitely going home with one of you tonight."

Ben exited to the left, where the rest of the bachelors had gone.

"You put us all to shame," one of them said. He was a doctor or something like that, and had been one of the first guys to be bid on.

"Nah," Ben told him. "They'd just had more to drink by the time they came to me."

The guys laughed.

"Speaking of our bachelors—gentleman, can you come back out onto the stage?" the announcer asked.

"Hey, guys, I need you to line up on stage again," Megan said.

There was some groaning, but they did what she asked. Ben buttoned his shirt and tucked it back in. Megan handed him his jacket. "Thanks for what you did," she said as he followed the other men.

They were back on stage, the lights beating down on them. "Gentleman, we could not have done this without you. Let's give them a hand!"

There was a lot of clapping and plenty of wolf whistles.

"Take a bow, bachelors."

They all gave awkward bows and then high-fived each other.

"Okay, ladies. Once you've paid for your bachelor, an escort will bring him to your table. Don't forget our silent auction, it closes in an hour. I know I said that, but the hunkiness on the stage makes us all forget our own names. We'll be announcing the winners in only two hours."

"Whew. Glad that part's over," Ben said.

"Me, too. Did you see who bid on me?" Jake asked.

"Nah. Wasn't watching."

"It was the CO's daughter-slash-niece's table."

"Clarissa?"

"Yep," Jake said.

Ben couldn't help but laugh. He'd had to take Clarissa to a couple of events for the CO. She was a wild one. They'd actually become pretty good friends because he didn't put up with her drama. The CO thought she was a handful, but the truth was, she was confused about what was important in life. All she really wanted was to find the right guy. Even, as she'd told him, if she had to date a couple of hundred to find him.

She might have something there. There weren't many people who could get along with someone like her. He wasn't attracted to her, which was probably why the CO had stuck him on babysitting duty for a few weeks.

"Good luck with that," Ben said.

Everyone knew the CO's daughter-slash-niece was

way off-limits. That was unless you wanted to be stationed in Antarctica.

"Hey, handsome," Ainsley said from behind him. "You were fantastic up there."

He turned and nearly bumped into her, she was so close. His hands rested on her forearms to steady himself. Her soft skin made him think of touching more of her and…

*Focus.*

"Thanks for getting that woman to bid for me, but that was a lot of money."

She laughed, the sound sending heat through his body. "We actually bid on you as a table. So you don't have one date tonight, you have ten."

*Wow.* "How does that work? I thought I was supposed to take someone on a date or something."

"Sorry, Megan and I should have clarified it for you sooner. Actually, the dates should happen tonight, here at the event. Takes the pressure off the guys having to plan something else. The bachelor basically dines with the lady that bid on him, dances a bit and that's it.

"But some of the higher bidders did it as a table. So the guy, like you, has to hang out at the table, dance a little, if you want to with us, and then you're done."

Well, that was a relief. He'd been worried about taking some woman he didn't know out on a date, especially someone from this crowd where money didn't seem to be a problem for a lot of them. He'd been wondering if Ainsley might come from money, given the fancy gown she wore and the fact that her sister was covered in diamonds. At least, they sparkled like real diamonds. Maybe it was costume jewelry. But then, he'd remembered how Ainsley had been dressed at the toy store, and even her casual look at the craft fair was pretty classy.

"Is it the same way with my table?" Jake asked.

"Yes, they also bid as a table."

Jake blew out a deep breath. "Saved."

The guys shared a look.

"What is that about?" Ainsley asked.

Ben shrugged. "Our boss's daughter is the one who was doing all the bidding. She can be a, um, handful."

"You said it, brother," Jake said. "So she has to share. That's a good thing. What I do not need right now is the CO ridin' my butt. You guys have fun."

"So, let's get you to the table. I'm your official escort." She tucked her arm through his. "Oh." She stopped and opened her hand. "I tracked down your tie. I promised Sandy—she caught it—that you'd dance with her later."

"Thanks."

A few minutes after that, Ainsley made the introductions. "And this is my mom, Carol. She's the one who jumped up to bid on you."

"Mom?" He frowned. "You can't be old enough to have a daughter of Ainsley's age and Megan's."

Her mom's hand fluttered against her chest. "From the look on your face, I almost believe you mean that," she said. "Either way, you made my night. Maybe even my month." The women all whooped.

"I do mean it," he said seriously. "I thought you

might be late thirties when you were bidding. Now I see where Ainsley gets her beauty from. It's very nice to meet you, ma'am."

He shook her hand.

"Yes, you are something special," her mother said. "Thank you for helping out Megan tonight. You and your friend were kind to show up at the last minute like that."

"You're welcome. That was a lot of money, though."

She waved a hand. "Oh, hon, don't worry about it. The women at this table were more than willing to keep you out of Steph Montgomery's hands. That was the table that kept trying to outbid us. I couldn't let that happen. She and her mother, well, it's tacky but they weren't winning this round."

"That's right," Megan chimed in. She'd come up behind her mother and was giving her a hug. "Thank you. We doubled what they did last year. I know you had a lot to do with that. You and your friends. And they're telling me that the bids on the auction items are already so high that we may even triple."

Her mother turned to kiss her daughter's cheek. "Our pleasure, dear. By the time that video finished, we were all in tears. That was brilliant of you, showing it at the beginning of the fund-raiser to get those purse strings loose."

Megan squeezed her mom. "I learned from the best."

Mother and daughter shared a smile. They must have done a lot of charity events together. All the women seemed very comfortable with one another. And he hadn't lied about Ainsley's mom—she was a beauty. The diamonds around her neck sparkled brilliantly. He was betting the necklace could pay for a house, or maybe two. Once again it hit him that Ainsley came from all of this. And here, he didn't even have a couch.

"We should probably feed him so he has the energy to dance," Ainsley suggested. "They've set up a buffet so we can grab some food before the music begins."

*Crud.* The dancing. "Uh, just so you ladies know, I'm not exactly the world's best dancer. I haven't actually broken any toes, but I've come close," he admitted honestly.

"You'll be fine," Ainsley assured him. Then she stood on her tiptoes and kissed his cheek. "You really are amazing for doing this," she whispered.

For that he would have done anything. The kiss was like a slow burn on his cheek, spreading through his nerves like wildfire. All the anxiety he'd felt earlier in the night fled.

"Anything for—" He'd almost said *you*. Would that scare her off altogether? She'd said more than once she didn't want anything serious. In fact, neither did he, so it was best if he kept this light. "The kids. Anything for the kids."

"Such a good guy," Ainsley said. "Let's get some food in you. You're going to need all your energy tonight."

It was how she said it that made him do a double take.

They were a few steps ahead of the others.

She smiled but didn't look at him. "Those abs were impressive. I might like a little alone time with them."

"So are you saying you want to touch them?" He'd always been direct and wasn't into games.

"Yep, all over."

He laughed. "Well, at least you're honest. What happened to not wanting to date?"

"I didn't say anything about a date. I just want to run my hands across those abs more than I want to breathe."

He nearly tripped.

"It's bad for me to objectify you," she said. "But those abs mixed with that big heart of yours is kind of my kryptonite. Just sayin'."

"Ainsley, you can objectify me all you want. Over and over again."

She sucked in a breath and fanned herself. "Marine, you cannot say things like that. I might melt into a puddle at your feet."

His mind flashed to her down on her knees in front of him. *No. No. No.* He had to get that out of his head. She was just flirting and having some fun.

"Hey, Ainsley, stop hogging the Marine," Megan called to them.

"Yeah," a chorus said behind them.

Then there were gales of laughter.

"Your ladies await," Ainsley told him and made a show of curtseying. Then she waved her arm in a regal manner to the rest of the women from the table.

He'd play the gentleman and make them all feel like they'd gotten their money's worth.

But there was only one lady he was interested in.

And he couldn't wait for her to touch his abs.

# 4

AINSLEY HAD WAITED patiently for more than two hours for her turn to dance with the Marine. Her mother's friends had helped pay for the privilege to have him at their table, but they were all a bit too handsy for her comfort.

Not that she should in any way feel possessive.

But she did.

Right now he was dancing with Sara Reyes, who was batting her eyelashes at him. The woman was her mother's age.

"If looks could murder," Megan said beside her.

"Shut it."

Megan laughed. "I thought you'd just met him."

"I did. I told you, at the toy store."

"Yep, but I've never seen you look at a guy like that. Ever. Not even Joe What's-His-Name when you were twelve and Mom took you to his concert."

Joe What's-His-Name had nothing on Ben. She hadn't been lying about his abs. When he came out from that curtain with his shirt unbuttoned, she'd squirmed in her seat along with every other woman in the place. Ripped. That's what he was. And there was a tattoo over his heart she was dying to explore.

Her body warmed again just thinking about it.

Fingers snapped in front of her face. "You do have it bad," Megan said.

Her sister had the most annoying habit of interrupting her fantasies tonight. First, on the way to dinner, and now this.

"What? I was thinking about work."

Her sister snorted. "Maybe workin' it. But that face…" She did a dismissive finger wave, clearly to tease Ainsley. "It's most definitely not thinking about work. He's so thoughtful. And one of the most gorgeous creatures I've ever seen. He keeps stealing glances at you like he wants to eat you up. I say go for it. Have a good time."

That's all it could be. She was sticking to her guns when it came to men, especially right now. While her parents might want her to marry and settle down, that wasn't a part of her plan. Not for a long time. It didn't matter how many men they paraded in front of her, or forced her to sit with at dinner. Their manipulation wouldn't work. They thought they were doing what was right—finding her a man who could take care of her—but she could take care of herself.

"I'm not interested. I keep telling you that," Ainsley said resolutely. "My business takes up my days, nights and weekends. We're doing really well. He's a nice guy who did us a big favor tonight. Leave it alone, okay?"

Then she gave her sister the glare. The one that said *if you push any harder, I'll tell Mom and Dad on you.*

Her sister held up her hands in surrender. "Fine. Fine. But just be straight with him. Tell him that you want to hang out, nothing serious. I bet he'd go for it. And from what he said about teaching and being a helicopter pilot, it sounds like he's kind of busy, too.

"He was saying they sometimes leave at a moment's notice for training exercises all over the world. This could be great. You don't have to marry the guy, although I'd love to see Dad's face with that one. Can you imagine? He'd probably have a coronary. I'll be honest. If you aren't interested in that Marine, I am. I'd be all over him like—"

"Megan!"

"Yeah, you aren't possessive at all," her sister teased.

"What's so funny?" Ben asked, approaching them.

"Girl stuff," Megan replied quickly. Ainsley was grateful for her sister's vague answer. She prayed he hadn't heard their conversation.

"Would you like to dance?" he said to Ainsley. The poor guy had been on his feet for two hours straight, wobbling through two-steps and waltzes, and a few fast dances with the other women at the table. He always seemed attentive and incredibly kind.

The way he treated others, it was like an aphrodisiac to her. Who needed oysters when Ben was in the house?

He was one heck of a hot guy. "Absolutely, but why don't you sit down for a little bit and rest. We've kept you running all night."

"I'm good. Besides, this kind of running is a lot easier than the obstacle courses on base. Afraid I'll step on your toes?" He moved by her mother's chair so she didn't have to twist around. And then he held out his hand.

"Not at all. I've been watching you all night. I've danced with a lot worse." She took his hand and then stood.

It was a slow number, thankfully.

As they hit the dance floor, he pulled her close and she put her arms around his neck. His went around her waist. With everyone else, he'd been quite formal. She liked that he treated her differently. Special.

"Been waiting for this since I got here tonight," he said. "Holding you like this."

She tipped back her head so she could see his eyes. She was five-seven and he had at least a good six inches on her.

"I said it earlier, but you've been such a champ. Every woman at that table has a thing for you, including my own mother. She keeps talking about you to her friends, about how you saved the day."

He chuckled. "How about you? Do you have a *thing* for me?"

She shook her head and he frowned.

"No. I mean, I do," she answered. "I mean… Oh, I'm making a mess of this. I told you what my life is like. I don't have time to have a *thing* for anyone. My schedule is insane. Crazy busy."

He shrugged. "This is how you let guys like me

down easy, right? I get it. You're out of my league. It's okay."

"No, you're not. If anything, the opposite is true. I just don't want to lead you on or set up some kind of expectation. And so we're clear, I want you. I just probably shouldn't."

"I told you before, I'm okay with getting to know each other. No pressure."

She smiled. "Guys always say that, and then they wonder why I'm not available twenty-four seven. I mean, I know I'm projecting. But the last couple of guys I dated—you're nothing like them. I get it. But I don't want to set up any false expectations. I pretty much live for my next appointment. Tonight is a luxury I don't normally allow myself. But it's for a good cause, and I've made some excellent networking contacts. Plus, we helped the kids, so it's all good."

"Uh, I don't have any expectations," he said. His brows drew together. "I simply want to spend some time with you. Maybe where we aren't in a store, or in a fancy ballroom with two hundred very loud women."

She'd noticed that he'd rub his temples now and then. Did he have a headache? Was the noise getting to him?

"Are you okay?" She was worried that maybe he'd been suffering all night and she hadn't been aware.

"What? Why would you ask that?"

"You were rubbing your head earlier. And Megan told me she was worried you were having a panic attack before you came out, but then you strutted down that catwalk like you owned the place, so she figured that maybe you were just preparing."

He pulled her tighter, and she liked feeling him pressing into her. She liked it a lot. "I'm fine. Sometimes noise gets to me a little. It's not that big of a deal. Though, I could have used some ibuprofen a couple of hours ago."

Oh, no. He didn't feel well.

The noise, between the music and the chatter, had been deafening most of the night. Poor guy. And he'd acted like it wasn't an issue.

"Would you like to take a break? I know somewhere we could go and it's quiet."

He raised an eyebrow. "What about your mom and her friends?"

"The party is dying down. They'll be fine." She hadn't lied. Most of the attendees were gathering their things. "If it makes you feel better, we can go say a quick goodbye. I'll tell them I'm the one with the headache and you're taking me home. What they don't know is home is a lot closer than they think. In less than five minutes, it will be superquiet and I also have something for your head."

He let go of her immediately. "Really? A couple of aspirin or something and even twenty minutes of quiet and I'll be good as new. That's a great plan. Let's do that."

This time she was the one who chuckled.

They said their goodbyes quickly, although she felt like her mom might have held on a little too long when she'd hugged Ben, but soon after they were headed out of the ballroom.

He started to lead her to the front of the lobby, but she grabbed his hand.

"This way," she said, pulling him to the elevator.

He frowned again. "I thought we were leaving."

"No, I said I wanted you to take me home and I promised you quiet. I always get a room the night of this event in case I drink a little too much. So tonight, home is on the top floor of this hotel. Come on. We can raid the minibar. Dinner seems like a million years ago and I'm starving."

She had no idea what she was doing or why she was taking him up to her hotel room.

*Right. You have no idea.* Okay, so alone time didn't sound like the worst idea in the world. And maybe her sister's words about having a good time were sinking it. This guy wasn't like anyone she'd ever dated. He'd even told her that he had no expectations.

*And I really want to know more about that tattoo on his chest.*

"You're okay with this, right? Going up to my room?"

He didn't argue, just followed her onto the elevator. A couple women joined them and gave her knowing looks. She didn't care.

She was taking her sister's advice and was about to get happy with a hot Marine, or at the very least, kiss one.

The warmth coursing through her body didn't lie, though. It was looking forward to so much more.

# 5

THE ROOM HAD floor-to-ceiling windows that looked out on the beach. Ben walked onto the balcony to listen to the calming waves. He was curious if he'd missed some kind of signal because Ainsley was all over the place with them. One minute she was talking about touching his abs—which he was, for the record, perfectly fine with—and the next she was telling him how she didn't want to get involved with anyone. That she didn't have time to date.

And then she'd invited him to her room. So he could have some peace and quiet and raid the minibar.

Ben was more than a little confused. Usually he kept things pretty simple with women. They had a good time, slept together and then that was that.

With Ainsley, well, it was complicated.

But he did welcome the quiet. He was embarrassed that Megan had told her about his breathing exercises backstage. That was something no one, except some of his closest friends, knew about. The waves were a lot more relaxing than the sounds in the ballroom and his shoulders felt like they'd dropped at least an inch, maybe two.

Inhaling the salty air, he closed his eyes.

Heaven. This thing with Ainsley, whatever it was— he'd let her lead the way. Maybe she was just as confused as he was. Given how she'd acted in the elevator, he had a feeling she wasn't in the habit of asking guys to her room.

He heard the faucet in the bathroom turn on. She'd gathered some clothes and gone into the bathroom to change.

He remembered he was supposed to be finding them drinks in the minibar, which was better stocked than most of his friends' kitchens.

Certainly better stocked that his. He'd moved into his apartment right before Thanksgiving. Then they'd been sent to Germany for a training mission. And since he was hardly ever at home, except to sleep, he hadn't done anything with it, or bought much food. It was the first place of his own. For years he'd been living on base, or military housing, but he'd always had roommates. He preferred sending his money home to help out.

But last year, his mom had finished her nursing degree and had a great job. She refused to take his money, though she allowed him to contribute to his sister's college fund. She was also paying him back for the house he'd bought them a few years ago.

He didn't need the money, so he put it in savings with the hope that some day he might settle down and get a place of his own. But that was a few years away. He had his eyes on making colonel, so he had to focus on the Marine Corps for now.

"You were drinking champagne—do you want that or something else?" he asked Ainsley, who was still in the bathroom.

"What do you want?"

*You.* But he didn't want to sound cheesy or scare her off. Maybe she really was just being nice and giving him some peace and quiet before he headed out.

"I was going to stick with water since I have to drive home in a bit." He'd already had a couple of whiskeys. That was his rule. Two drinks and done. He never had liked the feeling of being drunk or out of control. Plus, he had enough trouble with headaches, so the last thing he needed was a hangover.

"Oh, uh…" She sounded unsure about something.

"What?"

She opened the door and stepped forward. She was wearing little flannel shorts and a long-sleeve pink T-shirt that came down to her hips. He turned around and headed back to the minibar, pretending to be interested in the contents.

No question, the woman was beautiful.

Those legs. He so wanted them wrapped around his waist.

"I thought we might hang out a little. I'm hungry again. I was going to order room service."

Food and hanging out. Well, if that's what she wanted to do, he was game. And there was never a time he couldn't eat.

"I could go for some protein. Do they have a late-night omelet or something?" He shut the fridge door. But when he turned he found her staring at his chest.

He glanced down at his shirt. Had he spilled something?

"I don't do this," she said, and then she bit her bottom lip. She was nervous.

"You're going to have to explain what *this* is, because I'm not really clear on why I'm here," he said honestly. Though her look was telling him something that he wasn't sure she was ready to say. "I'm a pretty straightforward guy. Just tell me what you want, Ainsley. Tell me why I'm here."

She fisted the bottom of her shirt, and then took a deep breath. "I don't just have sex with guys, usually. I, um, I have to know them, uh, you. But you're different. I want to be superclear about this. *This* is simply fun. Okay. Just fun."

"Got it. You don't normally have sex with a guy in a hotel room, someone you've recently met, but you want to with me?"

She nodded. "You know, I'm a confident woman. So I don't understand why this is so tough for me. Do you want to have sex with me? I mean, we were flirting—"

His mouth was on hers before she could finish the next word. She tasted of mint, and he had to have more. He backed up against the wall and she leaned hard into him, her breasts pushing into his chest.

Her tongue warred with his, and when he slid his hands over her butt and brought her against his hardness, she let out a sweet little moan.

The woman was supremely sexy.

It was tough, but he broke off the kiss and lifted his head. "How does this feel?"

She blinked and then glanced back at his hand on her ass.

She nodded. "This feels good. Amazing. Spectacular. More. If this is our one night of fun, I want us to make the most of it. I need you to touch me almost more than I need to breathe." Her hand caressed his chest through his shirt. "Give me more, Marine. Much, much more."

"Unbutton my shirt, Ainsley." She wanted quid pro quo, he'd give it to her. Though her touch might be more than he could take. He was already so hard.

She gave him a fake salute and did what he'd asked. Then she pushed the shirt off his shoulders and he let it hit the floor.

She traced the Semper Fi tattoo with her finger. He'd had it for years, the first thing he'd done after boot camp. The same boot camp that nearly killed him. When he'd finished the intense training, he felt as if he could do anything. He also felt as if he'd found a home. He was faithful to the Corps through and through.

"Now you," he said, and he lifted the hem of her T-shirt. She was naked underneath. "More beautiful than I could have imagined," he told her. His thumbs gently teased the tightening buds.

"So are you," she said, her hands gliding up his torso. Then she kissed him. The sensation of her mouth on his, combined with the feeling of her nails lightly brushing his stomach... Well, he very nearly lost it.

Her hands moved lower, caressing him, and he hissed in a breath.

As much as he hated to, he gently took her wrists and put her hands on his shoulders.

"If this is going to last more than five minutes, I need you to keep your hands up here," he said, tapping his shoulders, before kissing her again.

She ground her pelvis against him, which wasn't helping him maintain his control. She needed a release and he was going to give it to her.

He rubbed her intimately, her shorts still on, but she quickly seized his hand and slipped it inside underneath them.

*Well, okay then.*

When his fingers found her slick heat, she groaned. At his tender touch, her body shook. Closer and closer still, she was reaching for that sweet release. Harder and faster, he aroused her; she now rode his fingers as if her life depended on it. He opened his eyes to watch hers glaze over.

"Ben," she whispered. "There. Yes. Right there." He increased the pressure and soon she was chanting his name. Her body was so responsive, it made him want her even more. He wasn't even sure that was possible.

She writhed and repeated his name, her cry sounded, her pleasure peaked. He waited for her breathing to calm—he had a feeling if he let go of her, she would fall. Remembering what she'd said about being a puddle, he smiled.

He walked her over to the bed and carefully laid her on it. It was high off the floor, which was perfect.

Soon, he was out of his pants, but not before re-
trieving a foil packet from his pocket. Marines were
always prepared.

Leaning next to her, he caressed her cheek and
kissed her lips, her cheek...

"Ben, I need you." She raised her arms and opened
them, welcoming him.

The trust she showed him was an aphrodisiac if ever
there was one. A man could get lost in those beautiful
green eyes of hers.

After putting on the condom, he spread her legs and
wrapped one around his waist, the other he left down.
He slid his tip into her.

She shifted, and used her leg for traction, easing
him farther inside her, moaning as she did.

He couldn't help but smile. He pulled out and then
pushed back in gently.

She bucked against him. "I need you, Ben. Fast,"
she said. "Please."

That confident woman he first met, the one who
seemed to own the world was back. She was no longer
hesitant, and he found it attractive. Oh, yeah, he was
going to give her whatever she wanted.

He pumped into her strongly each time and picked
up speed, biting his cheek as she lifted that other leg
and locked her feet behind him. She was fisting the
sheets, and from how she tightened around him, he
knew her climax was close. He put a thumb on her clit
and she arched off the bed. He'd barely rubbed it before
she was quaking around him, her muscles squeezing
him. It only took him a few strokes and he came hard.

He collapsed over her, careful to catch himself on his forearms so he didn't land his full weight on her. He kissed her as they rode the final waves together.

She touched his cheek lightly with her fingers. "That was fun," she said huskily.

"Yep." He wasn't sure how she could speak. His mind wasn't quite back on planet Earth. "Fun."

She kissed him. "I think we should do it again."

He chuckled.

"I mean, if you want to. And not right this second. I need food. But then. Then I want to do it again."

"Yes," he told her, though it was more of a mumble. "Again," he said.

"Good. Good. I'm craving waffles," she said, as she dropped kisses along his chest, lingering at his tattoo.

He didn't eat food like waffles. He was careful about what he put in his body, but he wasn't about to tell her that. She was so sweet, and hot, and sexy.

They talked about nothing and everything. A half hour later their food arrived and they discovered creative ways to eat it off of one another.

And then she said two words—"More, please." And he was lost in her again.

Insatiable, that's what he was when it came to her. But this one night was it. They'd both been clear about that, but as she climaxed around him for the third time, a truth became apparent.

He was in big, big trouble.

# 6

"Luv, you've been staring at that same screen for a half hour. The CEO from Wilson's will be here in twenty minutes." Bebe's voice broke through the haze that was her thoughts. Dang her. All morning Ainsley had tried to think of something other than her night of heaven with Ben. But—

"Ainsley! Bloody hell." She glanced up to find Bebe shouting from the door frame.

"How do you know I wasn't working?"

Her friend rolled her eyes. "People who are working make clickety clack sounds with their keyboard. Usually your constant rattle on the keys drives me bonkers. But today, you keep sighing and then nothing. Are you going to tell me what happened this weekend? You've been acting weird ever since you walked in the door. And what's with the gutted look?"

Was she gutted? Maybe. She shook her head. No one, as far as she was concerned, would ever know what happened with her and Ben. It was a special night she was going to keep in her fantasies, probably for the rest of her life. They'd made love three times and her body still felt the effects, a wonderful soreness that she didn't want to forget.

Even though she had to. That was it. They weren't even repeating that night. If only she could get the image of the hot Marine out of her head.

He'd had to leave before it was light out; he needed to get to the base, and she was still mad because she'd barely been able to open her eyes when he was gone. He'd whispered something but she couldn't remember the words.

She'd pay big money to know what he'd said.

When she'd opened her eyes finally, he was no longer there. She'd wanted to make love to him one more time. Just to get him out of her system.

*Yep. That's why.*

Bebe cleared her throat.

She glanced up at her friend. "I'm on it, okay? You know how I am when I'm working on those creative problems. Sometimes I stare off into space. Go make the coffee or something, already."

Bebe quirked an eyebrow.

*Cranky.* "Sorry. Sorry. I'll make the coffee."

Her friend smiled. "Don't worry about it. I'm just giving you a hard time. I already know about your midnight shag with the handsome Marine."

"What?" Her hands flew out and nearly knocked over her coffee cup.

"Well, technically, I didn't know. I guessed, but you just gave it away." She held up a newspaper. There was a picture of her dancing with Ben with the headline Military Men Break Charity Records.

*Kill. Me. Now.* What would Ben think of that photo? She hoped he didn't mind being in the paper or linked to her. Sometimes she forgot about the fact that some people were interested in her life just because her parents were wealthy. But the story really did seem to be more about the charity. At least there was that.

"So we danced."

"Yes. And then what? You must have been snogging the heck out of that Marine," Bebe said. "Look at how he's staring at you, like he could never get enough of you. Whew. That's some heat, luv.

"*And* you've been starry-eyed all morning. So this is what you're like when you get some good sex! Quiet, and introspective. Those aren't two words I'd ever use to describe you. Maybe it should happen more often. Should I call the Marine for another session? He might be better than meditation or even yoga."

"Shut it." What if he'd seen the photo? Would he be embarrassed? And her expression wasn't much better than his. What had she been thinking right then? Because she looked like she was ready to rip her clothes off and have him… Well, she sort of, in a way, had been thinking exactly that.

*No. No. Don't go there.* He'd been doing her sister a favor and now here was his picture. No doubt it was online, as well. Would he get in trouble with his boss? He'd mentioned a couple of times how the officers were expected to lead by example and she didn't know what he might think about ending up on the social pages. A big part of her was too chicken to even text him to ask.

"Hmm. You are smitten. Fifteen minutes until one of our best clients arrives. You might want to at least look at your presentation, which I did just email to you. I think you'll like the gifts I picked out for the executive level."

"Bebe?"

Her friend turned back. "Yes?"

"I really do love you best."

Her friend and business partner grinned.

Ainsley downloaded the presentation and sure enough, her friend had outdone herself.

Her phone dinged, and she glanced down to see Ben's name flash across the screen.

Her pulse quickened and she might have gasped a little.

*OMG.* She hadn't expected to hear from him again. They'd both agreed. She reached down to swipe across the screen, but stopped.

There were voices in the outer office. Shoot.

Ben would have to wait. Even though reading his text was the only thing she wanted to do. This was why she couldn't do relationships, or fun in general. Life was too busy and she had to put all of her energy into her business. Spending hours mooning over some guy was not the best route to being productive.

That settled it.

Leaving her phone on the desk, she gathered her laptop and headed into the conference room of the old house where she and Bebe worked. She lived upstairs, and the bottom of the Georgian home was where she did business. The conference room had actually once been the front parlor. She'd inherited the house and had planned at first to use it as a rental, but when she moved back to Corpus from Dallas, she and Bebe fixed up the downstairs for their offices.

They'd kept the original style, but freshened up the place. It didn't have the opulence of any of her parents' houses, but that was one of the reasons she liked it here. This house felt like a home, not some museum where you couldn't put your feet up. Straightening her shoulders, she didn't bother glancing back at her phone. Even though she really wanted to.

It was strange that Mr. Wilson wanted to meet here at the office, but who was she to question him? Saved her the drive to downtown, since her house was in one of the quaint neighborhoods near the beach.

She pasted a smile on her face and entered the conference room. When he stood to shake her hand, the smile became real.

Mr. Cam Wilson III was wearing board shorts and a T-shirt with flip-flops. Not exactly his usual Armani.

"The waves up today?" she asked.

"Yes, as a matter of fact they are. Packery Channel Beach is reporting five-foot swells—not so big, but bigger than usual." He clapped his hands together. "We have twenty minutes. Show me what you got."

And this was what it was all about. Her business and the clients who depended on her.

"Five minutes, and I'll have you out of here. Wait until you see what we've come up with." Thank goodness for Bebe. Maybe she really should talk to her friend about giving her a raise. She'd saved her today.

She'd get through this.

And then she was going to read the message Ben had sent, even though she really, really shouldn't.

AN HOUR LATER, she was in her car, still not sure what to do about Ben's text or where she was going. He'd texted I need an emergency gift. Can you help me out? Call me. Please.

It was business. She had to call him back, right? This was dumb. And he spelled all the words out. She liked it when people did that in a text. Half the time she struggled to know what people were trying to say. Megan only used emojis. Ainsley had yet to figure out what ice-cream cones, flowers and clowns stood for in a conversation.

*Just call him.*

She pulled into a grocery store parking lot because she didn't trust herself to drive, but before she could push the call button, her mother's number flashed across the screen.

"Hey, Mom."

"Hello, my lovely child. Where are you?"

"Heading to a client meeting." She was worried her mom would keep her on the phone for a while; technically, she was picking up lunch because she'd been so rude to Bebe about the coffee earlier and the guilt was still weighing on her. And she needed to get away from the knowing looks from her friend. Bebe shared Ainsley's intuitive nature, which was good for their business, but bad when Ainsley was trying to hide something from her friend.

"Oh, I was hoping we could have lunch before I head back to San Antonio to meet your father and some friends for dinner." Her parents had pretty much moved their base of operations to San Antonio two years before she'd graduated college, though her mom was in Corpus Christi at least once a month for a charity function or to visit friends. And they'd kept their house on Ocean Drive in Corpus. The monstrosity sat empty most of the time.

"Sorry. Crazy day ahead. It's my—"

"Busiest time of year. I know, dear. Are you going to be coming up for your father's football party this weekend? I can't remember which game it is. Anyway, he had some people he would like you to meet."

That was code. By people, she meant eligible bachelors. Ones who were well pedigreed, and probably boring, or really narcissistic jerks. She never liked to generalize, but the men her parents thought appropriate would never be her type.

If she had a type. Which she didn't. But if she did, it might be Ben.

No. Not Ben. Why couldn't she get it together? It wasn't as if she'd never had sex before—just not like that.

"Ainsley? Did you hit a bad cell area?"

She had to stop thinking about him. "No, I'm here. Was just checking my phone. Sorry, no can do. Busy, busy this weekend." That wasn't a lie. Her parents, or more specifically, her father, didn't see her business as something relevant. He thought it was more of a hobby for her. Her father didn't understand why she couldn't drop everything when he expected her to be around.

"How about the Christmas party? You're not going to disappoint us, are you? The whole family will be there, and won't your busy season be over by then?"

Not exactly. The last few hours before the holidays were insane. Last year, they were still dropping off presents at midnight on Christmas Eve, mainly for men who had somehow forgot to buy a gift for their significant others. How did you forget your partner? It didn't say a whole lot about marriage.

There was no getting out of her parents' holiday party, though. It was a family tradition, and they always had their big family get-together the next day. That part she liked. The party, not so much. Despite the decorations, drinking and general merriment, it always seemed a bunch of people trying to kiss up to her parents.

"Of course, wouldn't miss." And she'd already made plans with Bebe to hire some part-time staff to help them with the last-minute deliveries.

"Lovely. I'll tell your father you can meet his friends then. Bye, darling girl."

"Bye, mom."

Oh, well. Maybe she could find a date for that party. That would show her dad. She'd never understood why he raised her and her sister to be decisive, independent women, and then he wanted to pair them off with the nearest available bachelors. Correction, the nearest

available well-connected and usually shallow bachelors.

She loved her dad, but she was tired of the game
he'd been playing the last two years.

A plan began to form in her brain.

She couldn't. No. It was so very wrong.

Oh, but she was so going to do it.

# 7

BEN HAD MADE a deal, and he always kept his word. As he pulled up in front of Ainsley's office, he couldn't for the life of him figure out why his palms were sweaty. She was kind and beautiful and there was no reason for him to be nervous.

She'd offered to get some gifts together for him to pick out for the CO. All the officers had chipped in, and because he'd lost that original bet, he was still having to find presents for several events they had. Two more and he was done. But the next one was the CO's annual holiday party on Friday night. The whole platoon had been invited, and that was when the officers gave the CO their gift.

He'd wanted to ask Ainsley to the party, but she'd made it clear Saturday had been a one-and-done kind of night.

The problem for him was he wasn't done. It was hard for him to concentrate while at work. At odd times during the day he'd wonder what she was doing. And then at night, yeah, he couldn't think about that, either. No way he was going into her house thinking about the constant hard-on he'd had after their fun on Saturday night.

He could do this.

He double-checked the address on his phone, and then glanced up at the two-story house. It was white brick with shuttered windows and a large porch across the front. The door was painted a dark blue, the same color as the shutters. It was fancier than he'd expected. Her business must have been doing very well. Or maybe she shared the place with several other businesses.

She answered on the first knock. And darn if she wasn't the freshest thing he'd seen all day. Her hair was piled on top of her head. She didn't have a bit of makeup on, and she was dressed in a tight red skirt and white blouse, and was wearing glasses.

A librarian fantasy sprung to life in his head. He wasn't sure he'd ever fantasized about a librarian before, but Ainsley did those sorts of things to him. All the time.

"Oh, it's you," she said, frowning. "You're early."

Not exactly the welcome he'd hoped for. Well, that settled it. She wasn't interested in anything but business. And not the going-to-bed business he'd had on the brain for the last two days.

She glanced down at her phone. "Nope, I'm running late. Sorry about that. Come on in."

He followed her into the foyer, where there was a stairway to the left. "This is your business?"

"The downstairs is. The upstairs is where I live. Let's go into my office." Her black high heels clacked along the hard floor, and he remembered those legs being wrapped around him.

*Dude. You've got to stop that!* "It's very nice," he said, trying to act normal. What was wrong with him? So she lived in a nice house. Didn't matter. He was here to find something for the CO's gift, and then he was gone.

"I have some executive items for you to see. You mentioned your CO likes golf, which makes this a whole lot easier. One of my dad's companies makes all kinds of golf accoutrements. He has some new products that are going to be out in the spring catalog, but I have several of them. And then I have other gifts that might work if you don't feel like those are appropriate."

"You live upstairs?"

She turned and smiled at him. "Yes. Cuts down on the commute time in a major way. The house was kind of dated when I got it, so Bebe and I fixed it up."

"Bebe?" Why was he only asking questions? Because she was so strikingly beautiful he couldn't think straight.

"Oh, I keep forgetting she wasn't at the auction the other night. She was visiting her mom in Fort Worth. She's my business partner and best friend. She started out as my assistant but we soon learned she was really good with the finances. Way better than me about budgets and making sure we got paid.

"She is also great with the clients, so we both do a little bit of everything. About six months after she started, I asked her to become a partner. We say that means half the headaches are hers. And I'm rambling. I tend to do that when you're around."

Good, he made her nervous, so maybe it wasn't just him.

He followed her into her office. It was girly, with soft blue-gray walls and mostly white everything else. But it was classy, it fit her. There were pink flowers on her desk. And touches of pink around the room.

"You like pink?" Wow. He had to stop with the twenty questions, but he couldn't. Seeing where she worked, well, he wanted to know more about her.

"Yes. It's bright and happy. And I know, it's a little girl's color to most people. But I love it. For me it's a neutral. It goes with so much."

"It's my sister's favorite color. She's seventeen, and she's liked it, hmm, I'm pretty sure since birth."

Ainsley pointed to a side table. It was painted white like her desk. "Well, I promise you'll find no pink in the gifts I picked out for your boss." Right. This was about business.

She showed him a variety of products, including a putting machine that seemed tailor-made for the CO's office.

"Choosing was easier than I thought it would be," he said when they were done. He was disappointed because now it was time for him to leave.

"I'll get it wrapped and to you before your event, when did you say it was?"

"Friday." This was the perfect opportunity for him to ask her to go with him.

"Okay. Friday. Great. No problem," she said. "Will that be cash?"

He paid for the gift, and then put his wallet back in his pocket along with the receipt.

"Guess I should go," he said.

"Oh. If that's what you want, sure." She acted like maybe she didn't want him to leave.

This woman was the queen of mixed messages.

"There was something—" They'd said the same words at the same time.

And then there was a bit of nervous laughter.

"You go," he said.

She shook her head. "No. Go ahead. What did you want to ask?"

"Right. Like I said, the CO's party is Friday night. And I was wondering…"

"Yes?"

"If maybe you could help me find a date? I get that it's kind of last-minute. But I don't know that many people in town. And…"

"You want me to *find* you a date?" Her face fell. She was upset.

Wait. What did he say? *Find him a date.* Not what he meant.

Retreat. Retreat.

He'd just had sex with her on Saturday night. "I wanted to ask you," he said quickly. "That came out wrong. Not what I meant to say. I meant, I'm trying to find a date. I know you said you weren't interested in seeing me again. I think your words were 'one and done.'"

"Yes. That is what I said." She chewed on her bottom lip. He had the urge to kiss it.

*No. Focus.*

"And it would be as friends because, as I explained the other night, I don't really date. I'm concentrating on my career. But if I show up alone, I'm going to get stuck with the CO's niece. You know her, Clarissa. She's nice but she—"

"I'll do it," she said quickly.

Well, okay. That was great. There wasn't anyone he wanted to be with more than Ainsley. And she hadn't punched him for the idiotic comment about her finding him a date, so there was that.

"I'll go with you. You know, as friends... To help you out. But I need you to do me a favor on the twenty-third. Do you have plans then? It involves going to San Antonio for an event."

He was still wrapping his head around the fact that she was willing to go with him to the CO's party. Well, she was doing it to give him a hand, but he wasn't about to say no to spending even more time with her. "What day was that again?"

"The day before Christmas Eve."

"Oh, I was going to Austin to see my mom and my sister for the holidays," he said. It was true. He hadn't been home for Christmas in years, and he'd promised his mom he wouldn't miss it.

Ainsley's face fell again, and she leaned back on her desk. "That's okay. I'll still help with your thing."

"Nah, you're being a champ about the CO's party. It's the least I can do to help you in return. As long as

I can leave sometime that night to get to my Mom's for Christmas Eve morning, I'm good. It's only an hour away from San Antonio, so it shouldn't be a huge deal."

She gave him one of those devastating smiles. But there was something else there. Maybe relief? "So, what's going on that night?"

"Well, um, it's my parents' Christmas party. They throw it every year."

He wasn't following. If it was her family, why would she bother having him there?

"And you need a date because…? I mean, I don't mind, but you ought to look in the mirror. You could have any guy you wanted."

She gave an unladylike snort. "You're sweet. My parents use a party like this, or pretty much any time I'm home, to put eligible bachelors in front of me. And I'm about to be a lot more honest than I should."

"Okay," he said, curious as to where she was going with this.

"My dad has terrible taste in men when it comes to finding a mate for me. Like, the worst. I don't know why he can't see that these men are mostly narcissistic jerks, maybe because he can be a bit of one himself. Don't get me wrong, I love him. He's my dad.

"But everything is about him. He has it in his head that I have to marry so I'm taken care of. What he doesn't understand is that isn't what I want. I can take care of myself. If I ever get married, and that's a big *if,* I will marry for love. Not a bank account. Or invitations to galas and the Riviera. Shoot. I did it again with the rambling. Sorry. I'm frustrated with my parents right now."

"You're still so young, I don't understand why they'd want to marry you off." He wasn't going to explore the reasons why every time she talked about being with someone else, he wanted to punch something. They weren't dating. He needed to get his head straight.

She shrugged. "It's that protective instinct, I guess. Dad started off poor, never had enough to eat when he was a kid. When it comes to his daughters, he's always wanted to make sure we're taken care of. But what he doesn't see is I'm a lot like him. I'm making my own way in the world. I don't need someone to take care of me."

"Isn't that what marriage is, taking care of each other?"

She pulled the pins out of her hair and then put it back up. He wished she'd leave it down. He wanted to wind his fingers through it and kiss her again.

"Yes. But, I mean, my mom is always trying to please my dad. And a lot of the guys I've dated expect me to drop everything for them. If ever I'm crazy enough to say 'I do,' it will be to someone who sees me as a full and equal person in the relationship."

"How is taking me to the Christmas party going to help you with your dad? I'm not wealthy. Your dad will see right through that." No way could he compete with the kind of guys she was talking about. And he was curious about her dad. It was obvious she was used to money. He'd seen that at the charity event the other night. Just how rich were these people? Not that it mattered to him, but it did make him wonder.

"If I show up with you, you're an officer in the military and respectable. A Marine, which automatically makes you superbrave, and we already know my mom likes you. With you there, my dad won't keep questioning me on when I'm going to settle down. The parade of men will stop, at least, maybe for that one night. Then I can go on avoiding them for another year. It's terrible, but part of the reason I don't go see my parents as much as I should is every time we're together, they have a guy they want me to meet. And I have to go to this party and I do enjoy being with my family the next day."

"I don't mind helping you, but you're a successful businesswoman, a grown, adult person. I mean, you can do whatever you want."

"Right? And when I'm ready to settle down, I will. I make my dad out to sound like an ogre. He's not. He's old-fashioned. For some reason, to him, marriage means I'll be safe. Protected. But I'm perfectly happy to take care of myself, thank you very much."

She was. But he understood where her dad was coming from. If he was honest, he was pretty protective of his mom and sister. What didn't make sense to him was that he also felt protective of Ainsley. He had no right to those kinds of feelings. They barely knew one another. "I haven't been around you for long, but you do seem smart and capable."

"Sorry for ranting. By doing this, you will help me out. No matter how capable I seem, every year it's the same thing. I'll even throw in finding gifts for your mom and sister. What do you say?"

He stuck out his hand to shake hers. "Buying for them is tough. Deal."

She wrapped her fingers around his, and the heat nearly scorched him.

They both stood there, staring at their hands.

"I should go," he said.

"Sure. Thanks for agreeing to my plan."

This was getting awkward. "No, I'm the one who's grateful. And the gift you found for the CO is going to save my butt."

There was another long pause, and they both stared down at their hands again, letting go when they realized they were still connected.

"I was going to order pizza," she said. "It's weird eating a whole pizza by myself."

She wanted him to stay.

"Sure. Um, pizza's great." Again, it was something he didn't normally eat.

"You don't eat pizza, do you? Or chili pies. You're a health nut. And here I thought you were pretty much Mr. Perfect."

He chuckled. "Being healthy makes me less than perfect? Not that I consider myself that."

"Oh, no. As far as I can tell, you're perfect. But I happen to have the worst eating habits ever. I admit it, I'm a fan of junk food."

He nodded. "I don't judge. But I have to be careful about what I put in my body. Part of it's for the job, but there are other reasons."

She cocked her head. "It obviously works for you. Those abs made the kid's cancer fund a good ten thousand, but can I ask what the other reasons are?"

He followed her past the staircase and down a hallway.

"My dad died when I was twelve from a heart attack. He was in his late thirties and had seemed healthy, but they learned too late that his arteries were clogged." He wasn't sure why he was telling her all of this. "When he died it was really hard on my mom. She'd been staying home with me and my little sister, who was only two months old. He was a chef in Austin."

She stopped so abruptly he almost ran in to her. Then she turned and gave him a hug. "That's so sad. I'm sorry for your mom. Did you have other family around to help?" She let go before he could even wrap his arms around her.

But he wanted to.

"Not really. Her family was in Wisconsin, and she never talked about them much. It was a long time ago," he said. Thinking about the past didn't do any good. It had been rough. At twelve, he'd become the primary carer for his sister so his mom could work. When he was old enough, he'd had odd jobs sweeping up, or cleaning out houses that had been abandoned for one of his dad's friends to flip.

They'd made it through, and that was all that mattered. Taking on that responsibility so young had helped make him who he was, and he was okay with that.

She stepped through an open doorway and into a

large kitchen, so large his whole apartment would fit in it. There were creamy white cabinets and stainless-steel appliances. The stove alone was probably a few months' pay for him.

"This is—"

"Ginormous," she said. "This was the one part of the house that had already been remodeled before I moved in. They knocked out a bedroom down here to create the extra space. It's maybe a bit over-the-top, but I like it. I just wished I knew how to cook because it's definitely a chef's kitchen."

"So cooking isn't your thing? Is that the reason you eat the way you do?" he asked.

She shrugged. "That, and when we were growing up my dad was into fitness. He still is. He's obsessed with the body being a temple and all that. Believes that a healthy body and mind are what led to his success. So I grew up on green beans and brussels sprouts. It's childish, but my bad food habits are probably a late reaction to that. Do you know how to cook?"

"It's in my genes. At least, that's what my mom says. When my mom got a job and was gone for long hours, she did her best to prepare what she could ahead of time, but a lot of the meals were left to me. At the start, a lot of the food came from cans. It was easy to fix, but I got tired of that kind of quick.

"And my sister was superpicky. Finding stuff she liked was hard, and we didn't have money to waste. I wound up spending less time on the sports channels and more on the cooking ones. I learned to cook off the Food Network."

At first, it had seemed like another unfair chore, but then he'd discovered cooking was relaxing. He could lose himself in creating dinners for his family, and he didn't even worry about all the stuff he was missing out on, like the football team or track.

Ainsley shook her head. "I admire that you did that when you were so young. I can't believe you were taking care of your sister when you were still a kid yourself. It's like when we were talking about what you did right after high school—I was such a spoiled brat in comparison. I was probably more worried about boy bands and wearing the right jeans."

He laughed and she joined in.

He tried to be jealous, but he couldn't. That was just sweet.

"Yep. I worshipped a bunch of those groups. I used to spend the majority of my days on fan boards just praying they'd show up and post something. It's sad, but true. For the record, they never did. And they never showed up on my doorstep, which I just knew if they understood how much I loved them, they would have."

Okay, maybe he was feeling a little jealous right then. "Their loss."

She slapped a hand on the counter. "Exactly. That's what I think."

"Funny. I never had a crush like that when I was young. Though, maybe when I was in high school. My sophomore English teacher, Dr. Hatcher, believed in me. She's the reason I love books. She could see I needed some extra help so she made me read out loud to her—and by made, I mean, I sat in her classroom during lunch every day. At first I hated her for making me miss my one free period during the day. But I loved the book. It was *To Kill a Mockingbird.* And after that one, I read *Catcher in the Rye.* And then she introduced me to fantasy and sci-fi novels and I was hooked."

"That's such a great story. I was lucky. I was a total nerd who loved school. And I had so many great teachers, except for Mr. Brown. He was my geometry teacher. Ugh. Triangles still make me cry. But the rest of my teachers, I just loved them."

"They do make a difference to a lot of lives. Dr. Hatcher did to mine. Books were how I kind of lost myself in other worlds." It had been one of the biggest blessings of his life.

"So, do you actually have food in that Sub-Zero?" He pointed to the gigantic fridge. "Maybe I could cook us something that doesn't involve artery-clogging pizza dough."

She waved a hand toward the appliance. "We keep it stocked, or Bebe does. She's like you—with the exception of the occasional sweet, she eats pretty healthy. You're welcome to take a look. And if you don't see anything, I can order from a different place."

He opened the fridge door. He found chicken, lemons and minced garlic in a jar. "I've got this," he said. "Can you maybe make a salad?"

"If you're asking if I can chop stuff without cutting off my fingers, probably."

After showing her how to cut vegetables so she never had to worry about her beautiful long fingers again, he went to work.

A half hour later the kitchen smelled of lemon and garlic.

"True story—if ever you get tired of the Marines, you could so be a chef. Your mom was right." She took her last bite of chicken. "This was better than any restaurant meal I've had in a long time."

He chuckled. "I was worried I might be rusty, since it's been a while."

Her eyebrows drew together. "Why?"

"I've been living on base most of my career, so I eat what's in the mess hall. They've made a better effort of trying to provide better, healthier food. Same as when we're deployed, although, depending where we are the choices can be restrictive for obvious reasons. So I haven't cooked much. I only moved into my own place last month and we've been away doing training exercises for most of that time. To be honest, my fridge doesn't have much more than the makings for protein shakes and grilled veggies."

She leaned her elbows on the breakfast bar. "I haven't wanted to be too nosy, but what exactly do you do? You fix helicopters, but you can also fly them?"

"I'm a pilot and I also teach pilots how to do maintenance on their aircraft as well as what to do in extreme situations. On the base, I'm a senior staff officer of the squadron. But we do things a bit differently here in Corpus."

"What do you mean?"

"We share the base with the Navy. We're a special squad. All of us do a bunch of different things. We're support staff for other branches of the military, as well as the Marines. What I teach specifically is emergency mechanics while in the field. So if the navigation goes out, or something is wrong with the fuel tank and the squad has to land in the middle of nowhere, they can maybe fix the problem and get out of there."

"That's impressive. You're pretty *and* smart—such a dangerous combination," she said.

He batted his eyelashes and did fluttery fingers on his cheeks. His sister used to do it while singing Disney songs at the top of her lungs. "You think I'm pretty?"

"And I forgot funny." She was nearly bent over laughing at him.

She straightened and tried to be serious. "Thank you for dinner. I can't remember the last time I had such a good time." Her hand landed on his chest and the heat seared through him. He took her hand in his and kissed her knuckles. There was a connection, and while they might dance around it, there was no denying it.

"I'm not much for games," he said as he let go of her hand. She didn't pull away—in fact, she twisted her fist in his shirt. "And I'm not much one for pretending."

She leaned into him then, lifting her face until their eyes locked. "What do you mean?" Her words were barely a whisper.

"I want you."

"I want you, too."

"Then I'm giving you three choices. Take off your clothes right now so I can bend you over this breakfast bar and make love to you. Show me where your bedroom is so I can make love to you there. Or I'll sit in that comfy living room chair and you can straddle me."

She blinked.

"Pick one."

Her tongue teased her top lip. She glanced at the breakfast bar, and then back at him.

"Here is good."

# 8

"STRIP," HE ORDERED. They were in the middle of the kitchen and he wanted her. Here and now. Never in her life had she been more turned on. This night was so much better than she could have ever imagined. He was hot *and* he cooked.

Cooked her. She was heating from the inside out, and couldn't get her clothes off fast enough.

"Someone might walk in," she said, but unbuttoned her blouse anyway. She wasn't about to let this moment pass by.

"Do you have a lot of clients show up at seven thirty at night? Ones who just walk in the front door?"

He had a point.

"Right. You're so smart, as well as built." She tossed the shirt over one of the bar stools.

"That's the second time tonight you've said something like that. I almost think you might want me for my body," he said as he pulled his T-shirt over his head.

Wow. She hadn't imagined those abs. They were as perfect as she remembered.

"Like I said, here is good." She reached back and unzipped her skirt. It dropped to the floor. His eyes traveled down her body, and his look sent a delicious shiver through her.

Thank the universe she had the foresight to wear decent lingerie. The azure bra-and-thong set had been a last-minute addition to her wardrobe.

She started to step out of the red Louboutins, but he held up a hand. "Leave those on."

"Um, okay. But only if you start stripping, as well." She pointed to his jeans. "More than the shirt."

He smiled and her body actually shook.

"I was hoping you might do that for me," he said.

He didn't have to ask twice. Her hands were on his belt, zipper and, soon, on his erection. No wonder she was still delightfully sore from the other night. He was so hard and his cock had hit all the right spots.

Before he could say a word, she kneeled down and began sucking him. She couldn't resist, especially considering the pleasure he'd given her after the auction. That and she really wanted him in her mouth.

His cock twitched.

He moaned and then whispered her name. His pleasure was unmistakable.

She glanced up to find him watching her and the look in his eyes made her body tremble.

She teased him with her tongue and then teased just the tip of his erection.

"Ainsley." He said her name as if it required all

of his control. As she increased the tempo, they hit a rhythm and she enjoyed every moan, every bit of his praise and encouragement. Suddenly, he pulled out and reached down for her to help her up.

"Lean over the bar," he whispered in her ear. She smiled and turned her back to him, heard the rip of the foil package.

His hand caressed the length of her spine. Then those fingers found her heat. She was ready for him, but he found that same spot, the one that only took a few strokes before she was shuddering and crying out.

Never had sex been this good for her. Mind-bendingly good. The kind that made her worry he may have ruined any other man's chance with her.

Before she could catch her breath from the orgasm, he pumped his cock into her. His fingers found her clit. He caressed, and teased, and all the time thrust harder and faster until she forgot to breathe.

It was pure, glorious sensation. And when his other hand squeezed her breast, causing her to groan again, she couldn't seem to find the words.

"So good," he said, as if speaking for her. She held on as tightly as she could, overcome by the sheer outright bliss she was experiencing. This was so much more than she'd ever felt before. Thanks to Ben. He was a gifted lover, a good guy, honorable, kind…something she didn't want to think too much about.

"You are perfection," he murmured in her ear. "Like you were made for me."

She couldn't agree more and pushed her ass out to meet him, to feel his thrusts deeper. The orgasm came then, sure and swift, with black dots swimming in her vision and every muscle tingling with satisfaction.

"Yes," he said, and didn't stop. His thrusts were strong, relentless. She was going to come again. It was too much, too—and then she was lost. He lifted her chin back toward him and he kissed her with such passion.

As he came, he moaned her name. The syllables vibrated through her. And never in her life had she felt so fulfilled. So wanted and cherished.

They stayed like that for a few moments as he trailed kisses along her neck and then her shoulder and down her spine.

She then turned around so that she could kiss him. "So sexy," he said against her lips. "I could barely hold on."

She pressed her mouth to his and then broke away. "I say you held on just fine. But maybe don't let go of me anytime soon because there's a good chance my legs aren't going to work. You seem to do that. I'm thinking you give new meaning to the phrase *weak in the knees*."

He smiled and she beamed right back at him.

"I should probably help you do the dishes," he said.

Dishes? Who could even think about dishes? This Marine had some stamina. She tilted her head toward his. "You cooked, and um…gave me the best orgasms of my life. Well, you did that on Saturday as well, so not to worry, I can handle the dishes."

"Hey! What are you doing in the kitchen? I didn't think you even knew where it was. It's weird. The house smells like real food. Food that hasn't been burned," Bebe called out from the hallway.

Ainsley stammered, her mouth refusing to work.

"I was at the store, and thought I'd drop off some snacks. Don't freak out, I bought fruit. You should try it sometime."

"No," Ainsley yelled.

"Ains, you've got to get some vitamins in you somehow."

"No," Ainsley yelled again as Bebe entered the kitchen. She did a full stop just as Ben unceremoniously tucked Ainsley behind him.

"I was trying to say don't come in here right now. I'm—"

"Bloody brilliant. You're shagging the Marine in the kitchen," Bebe said. "About time you had some sex. What do you know? Miracles do happen." Then she plopped the groceries on the counter and walked out.

"Uh," Ainsley finally said. "Sorry."

"What for? That chest of his is the best thing I've seen in years," Bebe shouted from the hallway. "Good choice, luv. Excellent choice. I'll see you tomorrow. Don't forget to put the almond milk in the fridge. And I'll lock the front door so you don't get any other visitors tonight. Toodles."

The front door slammed and Ainsley stood there mortified.

He turned to face her. "So I'm guessing that was Bebe?" He had a big smile on his face. The tension eased from her shoulders.

"I'm so sorry about that."

"Why? Funniest thing that's happened to me in a long time. It's not often I get caught with my pants down." And he did—still had his pants around his ankles. Thank goodness the bar hid the rest of his body, or her best friend would have seen a whole lot more than his chest.

"I'm never going to hear the end of this," she said as she wrapped her arms around his neck. "She's going to throw innuendos at me for the next week, maybe month. Heck, probably for a year."

He leaned back. "Are you embarrassed by me?"

She frowned. What was he talking about? "You? Of course not. You're the best thing ever. It's the situation of having been caught in my own kitchen with a man. I haven't dated in over a year."

"That's a long time." He pushed her curls behind her ear. Her hair must have fallen down. She probably looked like an unmitigated mess.

"Yep. Right now, it's business first, which is why I told you about my no-dating policy. And then, of course, I asked you to be my date. So you probably think I'm crazy."

"Not even close," he said and kissed her cheek. "Trust me on that. I need to clean up, but then I have a fun idea about how to do the dishes. You up for it?"

She loved how he didn't care that her best friend had caught them at it, or technically post at it, in the kitchen.

"Oh, I'm up for whatever you've got, Marine."

THE WOMAN WAS ADDICTIVE and that brought him up short. And she hadn't lied about being up for whatever he desired. She was as open a lover as she was a human being. He'd never met anyone like her.

They were in her bed watching Fallon. Well, he was watching. She'd dozed off after their escapades in the shower. Her bedroom wasn't as girly as he'd expected. The walls were chocolate-brown, the trim and furnishings white. Except for some pink flowers in a vase on one of the nightstands, that was it for frills. She'd said she liked to keep things minimal where she slept so there were less distractions.

But sleep wasn't in the cards for him, not with her next to him. She might be the best distraction he'd ever come across. The sex was… Well, he thought he'd known what great sex was. But with her, it was more.

And they couldn't do it again. They'd talked about that on Saturday. This was a fluke. A one-off.

The last thing he needed was a girlfriend. Between his duties as a major and all the extra work he was creating for the incoming crew of new grunts, he was busier than he'd ever been.

They'd joked after the shower that maybe they had this lust out of their system.

She snuggled into him. He had to go. Needed his space, to clear his head. He couldn't think when she was around.

"Hey," he whispered as he kissed her cheek. "I need to go home. I've got to be on base at oh-four hundred."

She blinked her eyes open. "You can stay," she said sleepily. "It's okay with me."

"Thanks, but I have to get ready for work in the morning. I wasn't planning on staying even this long."

She sat up and blinked again. "Oh, sorry. Sure, you should go. I didn't mean to keep you."

He'd hurt her feelings. Even sleepy she was apologizing for what had happened. That was something he definitely didn't want. What they'd shared was great. But that had to be it.

He chuckled. "Ainsley, I wanted to be here. This was amazing tonight. I just… Well, you understand better than anyone about work priorities." He felt a bit like a jerk. But he did have reports to finish, and he needed space. Otherwise he might say something he'd regret. Like, they should do this every night…

*Yep, definitely time to go.*

"I'll walk you to the door."

She'd need to lock the door behind him, so he nodded.

When they were downstairs, he kissed her. And it was hard to lift his head and pull away.

"Hey," she said and grabbed his belt loop. "Anytime you want to come over and cook for me, I'm good with that." Then she gave him one of her smiles.

"Is that so," he said, wondering if she meant what he was thinking.

"Yep. You know, so you don't have to eat alone or anything." She wanted to spend more time with him. Interesting.

He was beginning to speak Ainsley.

"You said earlier that you were hoping we'd gotten this," he said to her and pointed between them, "out of our systems."

"Is it?" she asked. "Out of your system?" She glanced away, as if she didn't want to hear his answer.

"No." He wouldn't lie to her. "How about you?"

She shook her head, and then grinned. "So we keep it simple, right? Friends with benefits. We'll be each other's plus one at a couple of events, but that doesn't mean we can't also have a little fun, right?"

For some reason, and he knew he should, there was no way he'd argue with her logic.

"How about tomorrow night? I'll make us something good."

"That sounds like a plan. And by good, you probably mean healthy. But when you cook, it's better. Maybe I won't mind so much." She yawned.

"I better go." He kissed her cheek and then headed out. He waited on the porch until he heard the lock turn.

It wasn't long before he was back at his place, and he flipped on the light. The stark contrast between Ainsley's place and his home hit him like a slap on the face. He basically had a recliner in the living room, and a bed in the bedroom. An old, beat-up dresser he'd had when he was kid was the only other piece of furniture he owned.

It wasn't as if he couldn't buy more things. He'd planned on it, but he didn't mind the sparseness. Still, it was a far cry from her house. He'd never be able to invite her over.

And there it was again, him wanting what he shouldn't—couldn't—want. Even though she'd made it clear that they'd keep things simple. They were merely helping each other out. That was it. Okay, along with the best sex he'd ever had in his life.

It was dangerous for him to think about more. Not that he wanted to. He was as married to his career as she was to hers. And he really wasn't sure he'd fit into her world. That reminded him, he wanted to look up her dad.

He pulled out his phone and typed in Ainsley's name. There were tons of photos of her at parties and galas. And then her father's name and his bio.

The dude wasn't just rich, he had an empire. He owned sporting goods stores, restaurants and an oil company.

Ben scratched his head. That confirmed it. No way would he ever be the type of man who could hold on to Ainsley. She wasn't just out of his league, she was out of his universe.

So, he was going to appreciate their fun. And after Christmas, well, they'd both be moving on.

And he was going to keep on pretending that wouldn't bug the heck out of him.

He wasn't going to sleep anytime soon, so he grabbed his laptop and took it to bed. After finishing his last report, he turned off the light and stared at the ceiling, thinking about Ainsley and her curves.

When his phone rang, he sat up straight. Years of training had him instantly alert.

"Yeah?" he grunted into the phone.

"Dude, open your door," Jake said.

His feet were on the ground before he even thought about it.

When he opened his door, Jake stumbled forward, looking and smelling pretty rank.

"What happened to you?"

"Don't want to talk about it. Please tell me you have coffee. I've got to sober up before going back to base, because the CO will make my life a misery if I show up drunk."

True. He took in his friend's rumpled appearance, and then checked the time on his phone. Three in the morning—they had to be at the base in an hour.

There was a cut on his right eye.

"Did you get in a fight?" His friend was more a lover than a fighter, although he could hold his own if need be.

"Man, you wouldn't believe me if I told you."

Ben headed to his kitchen and pulled out the coffee. "Try me."

"So, remember that dance teacher from the other day?"

He tried to remember her name but couldn't. "Yeah, you were going out with her tonight. Did she punch you in the eye?"

Jake leveled him with a stare.

"Fine, so what happened?"

"Turns out she had a boyfriend. Well, technically they were taking a break. Guy shows up at the restaurant. Punches me in the face, and then proposes. Who does that?"

He coughed to hold back the laugh because Jake was so serious. He also wanted to hear the story. His friend was right, this was something else.

"No clue. A jerk?"

"That's what I was thinking. I was ready to punch him back when she grabbed my arm. Begged me not to, and then told him yes. That she'd marry him."

"Wow."

"The whole time I'm thinking, why does she want to marry this violent jerk who just punched my face? She tells me she's really sorry, but she loves him. She just wasn't sure he loved her. Then she hopped up into his arms, and he carried her out of there. All kinds of messed up. I'm telling you, I probably dodged a bullet with that one. What a night."

Ben couldn't hold back. "You do know how to pick 'em."

He grabbed some ice, and then threw it in a plastic bag and handed it to his friend. "That will help with the swelling. So what happened once they left?"

Jake leaned on the breakfast bar, clearly dead on his feet. "Dude, you have got to get some furniture."

"Go sit in the recliner. I'll bring you the coffee."

"I paid for dinner, and then headed to the bar a block away from here. Tried callin' you but you didn't answer. Nine beers later, I decided maybe walking was better than driving."

Well, at least there was that.

By the time the coffee was ready, Jake was asleep in the chair.

Ben decided to let him sleep for twenty minutes while he showered and changed.

This was why he didn't date or get serious about women. It wasn't only about work. He didn't need the drama. The "why didn't you call me or text me?" messages. Having to make plans that would impress. Jake provided the perfect reminder of why it was probably best to keep things simple with Ainsley.

It wouldn't do for him to think they could ever be anything more than friends with benefits. Albeit very good benefits.

He needed to make that clear the next time they were together.

# 9

AINSLEY WAS LATE. Ben tried not to think about it. He forced himself to focus on Brody's story about putting something together for the baby's nursery, but he was bored. And a little worried. She had texted him about an hour ago apologizing for running behind. She'd had an emergency situation with a client, but said she'd be there soon.

He'd told her to just show up when she could, but now he was wondering if she would arrive at all. And that had to be okay, because she was doing him the favor. There was one problem, though—she had the CO's gift.

He was about to text her again, when there was a commotion at the door. He glanced over the crowd to see long, feminine arms holding a gigantic present wrapped in gold, with a big red bow in the doorway.

"Excuse me, guys," he said to the little group around him. "That's Ainsley. I'll be right back."

"I can't wait to meet her," Matt's wife, Chelly, said. "Mari says she's gorgeous."

Clarissa beat him to the door. *Great.* Who knew what the brat would say.

"Wait, you're here for Ben?" Clarissa asked as he stepped up to the door. He took the heavy package from Ainsley and then blew out a breath.

She wore a red dress that fit her figure perfectly. It had crisscross wide bands across her chest, and then flared out at her tiny waist. And she wore the red shoes from the other night.

"When people talk about stealing their breath, they're looking at you," he said honestly.

Her cheeks turned a deep shake of pink. He wanted to ask her to go back to her place and beg her to take him to bed. But he had to remember where he was.

"Thanks," she said. "I'm sorry I'm so late. I actually had to drive up to San Antonio to get the gift. It didn't arrive today like it was supposed to. Some mix-up at dad's office. And then I got stuck in traffic. But I'm here."

"So, I was the problem client," he said.

She smiled. "Yes. But I didn't want to worry you."

"I'm sorry you had to go through all of that for me. We could have picked another gift."

"Oh, no. It's fine." This time the smile didn't quite reach her eyes. He didn't know her well, but something had happened today that bothered her.

"I understand you're really busy and that was four hours out of your day that you probably didn't have to spare."

"Maybe you should let her come inside," Clarissa said. "That Chanel dress is terrific and it looks like it might rain." He stepped back so Ainsley could come in. The back of her dress swooped down, exposing most of her beautiful back. He shifted the present to hide just how much that turned him on.

"I remember you from the charity event. Wasn't your sister in charge of that?" Clarissa asked.

"She was the chair, yes. Hi, I'm Ainsley."

"Clarissa." They shook hands. Then she glanced over at him. "Looks like you're dating up," she said.

That woman. She was right, but you didn't make those sorts of comments in public. She had no filter, which inevitably made everyone uncomfortable at some point. He'd talked to her about it numerous times. He was one of the few people whom she actually listened to.

Occasionally.

"Clarissa!" he said. "Just because you think it, doesn't mean you should say it."

She rolled her eyes. "Whatever, Mr. Polite Manners. I simply meant that she's pretty and rich. You could do worse."

He sighed.

Ainsley was laughing, and this time the sound was genuine. "Thanks," she said. "But if anyone is dating up, it's me. This guy." She squeezed his arm. "Best man I have ever known. I'm definitely the lucky one. And he cooks. What kind of guy looks like him and can cook? I feel like I've won the lottery."

She sounded genuine. That gave him a sense of pride—that she enjoyed spending time with him. From what he'd heard about her dating past, she'd been connected with a fair number of jerks.

Before Clarissa could say something else controversial, Ben broke in and said, "Let me put the CO's gift by the tree, and then I have some people I'd like you to meet."

She waved goodbye to Clarissa and followed him. The house was very modern and stark, much like the CO. He preferred things to be neat, ordered. Most Marines did, but he took it to the extreme. The best part was the view that looked out onto the beach.

After dropping off the present, he introduced Ainsley to his friends.

"So where did you two disappear to the other night?" Jake asked.

The guy had not given him a break for leaving him the night of the auction. He'd been so caught up in Ainsley that he'd forgotten that Jake had hitched a ride with him to the hotel.

"Dude, I told you she wasn't feeling good so I took her home," Ben explained, trying to stop the conversation before it went much further. He didn't want everyone knowing his and Ainsley's business.

Before Jake could mention that he had to take a cab to Ben's house to pick up his truck, Ben whisked her away…and right into the CO.

"Sir," he said.

The CO smiled. "Welcome. So, who's this, Major?"

"Sir, I'd like to introduce you to my date, Ainsley Garrett."

The CO held out his hand and shook hers. "Are you having a good time?" he asked her.

"Yes, thank you. It's nice to put names and faces together. Ben's been talking about everyone."

The CO shot him a glance. "He has? I hope it's been all good."

She laughed and nodded. "Absolutely. It's fascinating what you are doing on the base. Certainly, he doesn't tell me everything. But it's interesting that your squad is working with other branches of the military."

"Have you told her all of our secrets?" The CO smiled as he said it.

"No, sir. She's just a good listener."

"Clarissa tells me that your dad is Ed Garrett."

Her smile disappeared. "Yes, he is."

"We've been in a few charity golf tournaments together. Known him for years. In fact, I was going to hit him up for that new putting prototype he was talking about the last time he was here."

Ben glanced at Ainsley and did an inner hallelujah. That was the first gift she'd shown him. She was very good at what she did.

She smiled. "Hmm. Call it a guess, but I have a feeling that when you open your present from your staff, you're going to be very happy."

The CO's eyes rounded. "Really?"

"It was Ben who asked if we could get one for you. And it's hard for me to tell him no. I drove to San Antonio today to pick it up from the factory."

"Good call, Ben. Come on. Let's open it," the CO

said. Never had he seen the CO behave this way. He was like a little kid.

They all shared a laugh together.

"Excellent suggestion," he said to Ainsley as they followed his commanding officer across the crowded living room. "And thanks for giving me all the credit, which you deserve. This might keep him off my ass for a day, maybe even a whole week."

He slipped an arm around her shoulders.

"It's my pleasure," she said. But she didn't smile this time. Something was bugging her.

Ten minutes later, much to the chagrin of Clarissa, they had the new putting machine set up in the middle of the party. All the guys were trying it out.

"You did good," Ben said. "I've never seen him this happy or relaxed. The guys and I owe you."

She frowned. "It's no problem." But it didn't look like it.

"What's wrong?" He was genuinely concerned. In the short time he'd known her, he'd never seen her do anything but smile.

She shook her head. "Nothing. Sorry. Just thinking about today. We can talk about it later."

He glanced around and noticed everyone was focused on the CO's new toy. "Want to grab some air? The deck is covered, and he has a great view from there."

She twisted her lips and glanced nervously through the windows. "If that's what you want."

What was going on?

The rain had stopped, but the wind had picked up.

He took off his jacket and put it over her shoulders. "Thanks," she said.

"You want to tell me why you're upset? I really am sorry about you having to take so much time to get the CO's present." They might be just friends, but he wanted to help if he could.

"No. Because this is nice. The party is great. Your friends are fun. I like the way you covered with Jake. Thanks for that. It's been a long day, and I want to focus on what's going on right now. Nothing else matters."

So there was something.

"I wish you would go ahead and tell me whatever it is that's bothering you. I know this is temporary, but I don't want secrets between us. Did you meet someone else? It's okay if you're having a hard time telling me."

He wasn't sure where that had come from, but it would explain why she was acting so uneasy. But his gut churned and maybe he didn't want to admit how much the idea unsettled him. *A lot.*

She sighed and leaned her hands on the railing. "No. It's complicated. I told you that I had to go to San Antonio to pick up the gift because the shipped one wasn't going to arrive on time. I'm not sure what happened with that. We ordered it in plenty of time and, hello, it's only an hour away. And after what's occurred with my dad, I'm not so sure he didn't have something to do with it."

"I really appreciate that you did that. I know how busy you are."

She nodded. "One of the main reasons I was late…

Dad insisted I have lunch at the club with him. And, of course, being my dad, he had this guy he wanted me to meet. I felt…weird. Like I was cheating on you. I mean, I know all of this is supposed to be temporary. We only met a short time ago. But I really like you a lot. And it just seemed wrong being there with him."

Dang if Ben didn't feel like throwing his arms around her. Okay. This was supposed to be casual, easy, but the truth was the last few days he'd been thinking maybe they should look at spending more time together. He wasn't exactly sure what *more* was, but he couldn't get her out of his head, and he had a feeling that wasn't going to change anytime soon.

"I like you, too," he said. "But it's not like you initiated the date, right? And even if you did, I'd have to accept that. We aren't really dating." It was hard for him to say, he realized.

"Yes, but I should have anticipated my dad doing that. And what bothered me the most was it did very much feel like I was cheating on you. I can't, that's… I'm just so confused. This thing between you and me, we're having fun, right?"

"Absolutely."

"But it feels, I'm not sure how to explain it exactly. I almost wanted to call you from the table and say, 'Hey, I had no idea this was going to happen. This guy is pretty much a blockhead. I'll be back as soon as possible.'"

He chuckled. "I get it," he said. And he did. They'd only spent a short time together, but they'd spent every night since Monday in her bed. Whether they wanted to be or not, they were connected. "If it makes things any better, I'm as confused about what's going on between us as you are. But in a good way."

She glanced up at him. "Really?"

He nodded, and then he turned so he could wrap his arms around her. "This thing between us is kind of intense."

"Kind of?" she asked.

He smiled. "Okay, it just is. So we see it through, right? Neither of us has much experience with relationships, or at least long-term ones. We don't have the time to maintain them. But we hang out, enjoy each other and see where it goes. Deal?"

"It's an exclusive deal, right?"

He thought for a minute, trying to figure out what she meant. "As in we only date each other as long as we're together?"

"Yes."

He shrugged. "I kind of thought that was implied."

Then she hit him with one of her devastating smiles. "Good," she said. "I was about to read the riot act to Clarissa. See how she kept looking at you like she wanted to eat you up? The only person who can look at you that way is me. Got it?"

Smiling, she poked his chest with her finger.

He smiled back.

"Wow. Who knew Ainsley could get jealous? I kind of like this side of you."

"That woman rubs me the wrong way," she said as she wrapped her arms around his waist. It was crazy how she fit him so well.

"She does that to a lot of people. You don't have to worry about her. I'm more worried about these surprise dates your dad keeps setting you up on. Now every time you go to San Antonio, I'm going to wonder."

She sighed. "You don't have to worry, either. You already know how I feel about all of that. And today, that guy, Todd, I think he was blindsided, as well. I doubt he had a clue what my dad was up to until I got there. He thought he was there to talk about a business venture. I felt bad for him. But he was a blockhead. He was nice to me, but only when my dad was looking. Not a very genuine type of person, to put it frankly.

"Have I mentioned my dad has really bad taste in men, when it comes to picking out one for me? Fortunately, that was the last time, until the Christmas party in a few weeks, that I'll see my dad. I now have the world's best excuse and I'm really good at using it. Work is crazy! Which reminds me, I'll be late tomorrow night. We're wrapping all the presents for Clinical South."

"At the house?"

"Yep."

"I could make you and Bebe dinner? I'm the world's worst wrapper, but I can provide sustenance."

She kissed his chin. "You're the best. As you find out more about my family, you'll see I'm not like them in a few ways. They love me and I love them. But I've felt like an outsider at times. Like I don't belong or I'm playing a part. That world isn't who I am. I'm just a girl who runs a business, and is into a really hot guy."

He squeezed her tight. "And I'm just a Marine. I'm

kind of a 'take me like I am' dude. But if you can deal with that, I can deal with the fact that your dad might not see me as a prime candidate for his daughter. I won't fit in that world, either."

"That's funny. Clarissa commented about my dress. But it didn't even register who made it. You told me the other night that you liked the color red, and I wanted to wear it for you."

This woman was special, truly. "Ainsley, you were wearing red the other night when I said that. I love any color you're in."

"You say the sweetest things," she said. "Oh, I actually do have a favor to ask you."

"Name it. I'm yours."

"Be careful with that," she said and winked at him. He loved when she did that. "This is more physical."

He couldn't help his smile. "Even better. I've proven getting physical is my specialty."

She giggled. "You are so bad. That's not what I mean."

He pretended to frown, and she rolled her eyes.

"When I was looking for ribbon earlier today," she said, "I found a box of Christmas lights and holiday lawn ornaments I'd forgotten about. I love having things all done up and festive, so I was wondering if you might put up the lights and decorate outside for me? I'd do it, but I'm afraid of heights. Bordering on 'having a breakdown' fear of heights."

Right. Well, the last thing she needed to be was on a two-story ladder. "I'd be happy to do it. I've got the

Toys for Tots drive in the morning, but if the weather clears I can do it tomorrow afternoon or Sunday."

"You are my favorite person," she said and then her lips were on his. Kissing her was nothing but sunshine. He couldn't get enough.

He lifted his head just as thunder hit. She jumped a little and he held her tighter.

"Are you cold?"

"Are you kidding? Every time you touch me I feel the heat. I've never—"

His lips were on hers before she could finish speaking. That heat burned within him, as well. The storm raged around them, but they were lost in their own world.

"Hey, Major, you know how the CO feels about PDA," Brody said.

She jumped away and then giggled. "You scared me," she said.

Their quiet alone time was over. They both turned to look at Brody. Ben's frown was for real.

"We're just talking about putting Christmas lights up on the house. Uh, Ainsley's house," Ben explained. There was no way to salvage the situation. They'd been caught.

"Hmm. That's interesting that you can still talk when your lips were together like that. Hey, I have an idea. If you help me with my lights," Brody said, "I'll help with yours. I had to buy new ones because suddenly Mari doesn't like all white, now she wants blue on everything. I can't keep up with her. She's nesting, and by nesting I mean she decides she wants something and then it's up to me to make it happen."

They all laughed. "Better not let her hear you say that," Ben warned.

"Say what?" Mari asked from behind Brody. "Step aside, Marine, I need some air. Look at that storm." She went to the railing and gulped in the fresh gulf air. "It's stuffy in there. Oh, hey, Ainsley. I didn't know you were here."

"Good to see you again," Ainsley said and let go of Ben so she could shake hands with Mari.

"Same here. That dress is gorgeous. Chanel, right? So amazing. Man, makes me miss my waist." Mari patted her pregnant belly, which was twice the size as it had been at the high school craft fair. Though Ben knew better than to say anything like that.

"Oh, you look gorgeous," Ainsley said. "Pregnant women have the most beautiful skin and hair. Even in the dim light out here you're radiant."

Brody came up, put his hands on Mari's shoulders and kissed her cheek. "She's the most beautiful woman I've ever seen."

Mari sighed. "And that's why I keep him around. Never mind that he had to help me put my shoes on tonight because my belly is so fat I can't see my feet anymore."

"Just more of you to love, baby," Brody said.

Some good-natured teasing ensued.

"We're saved, honey," Brody said. "Ben's agreed to help me with the Christmas lights if I return the favor and help with Ainsley's house."

"Oh, that's nice of you guys. I worry about him out there on the ladder by himself. He won't let me be his assistant."

"No way," Brody said. "You're getting nowhere close to a ladder, even if it's only to hold it."

"No prob," Ben said. "Happy to help out."

"Toasts are about to begin," Jake called to them from the patio doorway. "I should have known you guys would all be here making out."

"Jake!" Mari said. "We're talking about holiday lights. Would you like to help the guys tomorrow?"

Jake's jaw dropped as he realized he'd just walked into a trap. "Uh, I'm busy?"

"Too late," Mari said. "Brody will text you the details. Once you finish at my house, you're going to give a hand to Ainsley with hers."

"Fun times. Does anyone ever say no to you?" Jake asked Mari.

"Nope," she said. "And you're not going to start. I'm pregnant, so it's totally against the law to even think about saying no."

Everyone roared with laughter.

They traipsed back inside, but Ben claimed Ainsley's hand before they joined the others. They'd been interrupted. Well, technically, their kiss had been. It was a strange night, and he needed to make sure she was okay.

"We're good, right?"

She stood on her tiptoes and kissed him. "We're great," she said. "We'll be even better when you get me home and out of this dress."

Ben hissed out a breath. "You can't say things like that to me, especially in public." He pulled her against him so she could feel his erection. She wiggled into him.

"This is work, Marine, and you should probably be responsible and mingle. But I really wouldn't mind if in twenty minutes or so we said our goodbyes." She slipped her arms around him. "This dress is suddenly feeling way too tight. I can't breathe. I might be feeling faint. How are you feeling?" She slipped her hand between them, rubbing up and down his cock.

*Yes. Yes. Yes.* This was happening.

Desire crowded out any rational thoughts in his head. He couldn't think, period. They had to go. Like yesterday. "Goodbyes be damned. We're leaving."

"But my car," she protested, laughing. "I can't leave it here. That would look bad for both of us." The wind was whipping her hair. And the dress outlined her curves.

"Give me your keys." He sounded like he was ordering one of his students to do something. "Please. Sorry. Those words came out of your mouth and now I can't think about anything else."

She kissed him again and handed him the keys.

He leaned his head inside the doorway, noticing the party was in full swing. "Brody," he said because he was the closest.

"Yeah?"

Ben held out the keys. "Jake has to get Ainsley's car to my place. I'll pick it up tomorrow. Tell him he owes me. He owes me like ten times over."

Brody frowned. "Okay, what's up?"

*Crud.* He wasn't expecting an inquisition. "Uh, she's got a work thing, so I'm taking her home."

Brody glanced at Ainsley, no doubt noticing her flushed face, and then gave him a knowing look. "Right. She has a migraine. Got it."

They both smiled.

"You're a good friend," Ben told him.

"Yep, remember that tomorrow afternoon when you're at the top of that ladder sticking lights on my house."

Ben didn't care about tomorrow. All he wanted was to get Ainsley naked as quickly as possible.

# 10

BEN WOULDN'T LET her peek at what he'd been up to outside. She'd heard the guys laughing and thanks to him putting something in the Crock-Pot, the whole house smelled like yummy food.

She was starving.

They'd made love most of the night. She couldn't get enough of him. Then he'd brought her breakfast in bed. She kept trying to find ways to surprise him, or do little things for him, as well.

Like giving him a massage, but then that had turned into something for her because they'd ended up in the tub and wow. Yep. That had definitely turned into something for her.

"You two look serious," Bebe said as she finished up the last of the wrapping. The drill team had done most of the patients' gifts, but she and Bebe had wrapped the gifts for the staff and executive board for Clinical South.

"I told you. We're just having some fun." She couldn't

help the sly smile slipping across her face. Something had happened the night before. It wasn't just sex anymore. They'd made love, and it was intense.

Every time she thought about the way Ben looked at her as he came, tingles spread throughout her body. It was as if he'd committed to her in that moment, and she'd liked it…a lot.

"Right. The kind of fun where he's here every night. Cooks for you and puts Christmas lights on a two-story house for you. Where he stares at you as if you were the most beautiful woman in the world. The kind of attention that most women only dream of."

"Yep. That kind of fun," she said sheepishly. "We can't call it anything else. We're both being honest about putting our careers first right now. He wants to make Colonel sooner than expected. Did you know he made Major about six years ahead of time? He's such a hard worker and a good leader. Mari was telling me that Brody can't say enough nice things about him. It scares me that he's almost too perfect, and what experience do I have with that? None."

"Not that I have a lot of experience, either, with great relationships," Bebe said, "but I'm pretty sure love doesn't stick to a timetable."

"Love?" The word caught in her throat. She took a swig of water before she choked. "Oh. No. It's not serious like that. I mean, shoot. We've only just met, or rather, it's only been a week."

Bebe waved the scissors dismissively in the air. "Yes, love. Again, not really speaking from experience, however, you have to know that whatever you call it, it's special. Do you feel the same about him as you have the last ten men you've dated?"

When she put it like that, it made Ainsley think. "You're scaring me. Don't go there. I'm not joking. You'll freak me out. Why do people always have to put labels on things? Fun. It's just some serious fun."

Bebe gave a dramatic sigh. "It shouldn't scare you. If anything, you should be grateful and running toward the light."

Ainsley snorted. "This isn't some *Wuthering Heights* drama. Yes, it's something new for me. A man who puts me before his needs. Who supports my career. Wants the best for me. But I'm not rushing anywhere. I won't get tied up with any guy."

"Tied up. Hmm." The humor in Bebe's eyes was plain to see. "Tied up by the Marine? Interesting. I bet you're one present he'd definitely like to unwrap."

He already had. Many. Many. Many times. "Oh, stop it." Ainsley threw a bow at her. "Don't ruin this for me. Let me live in the bubble, at least until Christmas."

Bebe frowned. "What happens at Christmas?"

"We put an expiration date on the whole idea. But then, last night... Well, it's confusing. I'm just not counting on this being long-term."

"Nonsense. Do you actually believe what you're spouting? You can't schedule love or expect it to be there when you do want it."

"Ugh. It's not love!" She very nearly screamed the word.

"Ainsley?" Ben called for her.

*Shoot.* She hoped he hadn't heard her. "Shut it. And behave." She pointed a finger at her friend.

Bebe made the universal sign for a zipper over the mouth. Not that it would stop her.

"In the conference room," she called to him. "What's up?"

"Ready for your surprise?" he asked.

Bebe stood and made an explicit back-and-forth motion with her hips like she was having carnal relations with the curtains.

"You're insane," Ainsley hissed.

Then they both laughed.

"Yes," Ainsley said and rushed to find him. "I can't wait. I'm so excited." She caught up to him in the front entry.

He rubbed his hands together, clearly happy with himself. "Just so you know, Ains, I might have gone a little crazy. My engineering brain took over, but it'll be easy for you to use."

Now she was nervous. Her neighborhood had rules, and if he'd gone too crazy she'd probably get cited. If he'd put Rudolph in her yard or one of those giant blow-up Christmas ornaments, they were going to have to have a chat. And he'd been so sweet. She didn't want to disappoint him.

But she also didn't want to get fined by the home-owners' association.

She and Bebe followed him to the front yard. Jake was there, putting a ladder into his truck. "Thanks for helping out," she told him.

"No prob," Jake said. "We actually had some fun.

And it was interesting to see the way Ben's mind worked."

"How so?" Ainsley asked.

"Ben can do anything with a bunch of wires and some electricity. He's a magician. Wait until you see."

They all talked about how smart Ben was, not that she'd seen anything to the contrary. But he wasn't a showoff about it. They'd talked about books, the world, music, politics, but he was never a snob about anything.

"What happened to Brody?" she asked.

"Mari called, so he headed home. She's due any day, so it's better if she isn't alone a lot of the time. And she was hungry. I swear, I had no idea a person could eat so much."

"I guess it's true about eating for two," Ainsley said. Still, she believed Mari was gorgeous. "I hope she's doing okay."

Jake shrugged. "Brody didn't seem too worried. He's like a mother hen around her. So if he's not worried, I'm sure she's fine."

"Are you ready?" Ben asked. He was on the porch now, holding an iPad.

She nodded, curious to see what they'd been doing all afternoon.

He handed her the iPad. "I made it easy for you. All you have to do is push the button on this app. Go on, just push the button and you'll see."

It was silly, but her hand was shaking a little.

She did as he asked and then gasped. It was beautiful. He'd used white lights to outline the architecture of the house. The rooflines and windows, as well as the columns. They'd even wrapped the chimneys. Wreaths had been hung over each of the windows. It was simple and beautiful, like something out of a winter wonderland. It couldn't have been more perfect for the home if she'd designed it herself.

"I love it." She turned and threw her arms around him, squeezing him tight. "Amazing. It's everything. I can't even thank you."

On each side of the porch he'd put two Christmas trees with matching lights. It was a scene from a postcard. All they needed was some snow and it would be Norman Rockwell worthy.

Not that snow was a possibility in Corpus, unless it was the fake kind.

"I'm glad you like it," Ben said, looking relieved. He'd been worried she wouldn't like it? Oh, that made her heart beat even faster.

"I was kind of afraid it might be too much. But we were having a blast. The lights go off automatically at midnight. Or you can turn them off with the iPad. And they come back on at seven p.m. It gets darker in the winter. That way, you don't have to worry about it. I know how busy you are."

"Ben." She brushed her fingers across his cheek. "I'm so happy. You totally got me and what I wanted. You really are a true hero. But with wires, like Jake said."

"Jake, perhaps we should leave these two alone," Bebe said. "This looks like it could get X-rated soon."

"Shh," Jake said. "Let's just tiptoe away."

"Relax, guys." Ben turned her so they were both

facing the house. "I promised Mari we'd drive by their place later so you can see her blue lights. We used part of the white ones Brody had bought to finish off the roofline. He said there's no need to pay him since I helped him out. You've got a very big house."

"I can't believe all the work you put into this, and you did it in a few hours. It's wonderful," she said, starting to sniffle. *I will not cry. I will not cry. I will not cry.* It was all the kindness that was getting to her. It was one of the reasons she loved her business so much because it was focused on giving.

But Ben had given her the greatest gift. And he always talked about how busy *she* was, but he worked just as hard, and often more hours. A couple of times she'd caught him doing work on his laptop when he thought she was asleep, and he was up and at the base in the morning before she'd even thought about waking up.

"I don't think anyone has ever done something this nice for me." She hugged him.

He pushed her hair behind her ear. That was his thing, and every time he did it, she fell a little bit harder.

This man gave her all the feels.

"This was a new one for me. I've never had a house with Christmas lights. When I was growing up we lived in apartments. I got Mom the house a couple of years ago, but I can't remember if she decorates. Like I said, it's been a long time since I've been home for the holidays."

"You bought your mom a house?"

He shrugged. "I thought I told you that. She's paying me back. I don't want her to, though she insists now that she's got a good-paying job as a charge nurse. Anyway, I like doing things for you." His voice grew husky and then he stepped back.

He'd bought his mother a house. And this was his first time home for Christmas. It made her want to bake him cookies and put up a tree. Hmm, maybe not the baking. She was dangerous in the kitchen. But the tree—definitely. She was so taking him to buy a tree. And maybe one for her place, too.

She'd meant to ask him about his apartment. If maybe he wanted her to come there sometime.

"Jake wanted to put a giant plastic Santa on the roof, but I drew the line there."

She laughed. "Thank you for that."

"Hey," Jake said, jumping in. "There's nothing wrong with Santa. Santa's a classy touch."

"Yeah, dude, if you say so." Ben grinned. "Jake did have a good idea for later, that is, if you have time."

"I thought we were eating dinner?"

"After that," Ben said. "I know you aren't a fan of heights, but we thought it might be in keeping with the season to go and look at Christmas lights."

She frowned. "I'm confused. Why would I have to be afraid of heights for that?"

"We want to take you and Bebe up in one of the Apaches. I've got to get some flight time in this weekend, and it might be fun. Bebe, what do you say?"

Helicopter. Big sigh. She'd been in one in Hawaii, but it hadn't been her favorite experience. In fact, it was one of the reasons she hated flying in general. She did it, but she wasn't a fan.

On the other hand, Ben seemed so excited and she didn't want to disappoint him. And there was the fact that this was his work and he wanted to show it to her. Yup. That was just plain sweet.

*Suck it up.* She hugged him again to delay her answer. *Just say yes.* But she couldn't quite form the words. Sweat trickled down her back.

"I don't know about Blondie. She's not a fan of flying, but I'm in," Bebe said. "I've never been in a helicopter and certainly not a military one. Sounds like fun to me. And Christmassy. All these lights make me a little homesick for London."

Her mouth opened, but still the *yes* wouldn't come out. Ainsley usually considered herself brave. She wasn't afraid of anything—with the exception of helicopters. Planes, she could shut the window shade and pretend she was in a safe tiny capsule. But with helicopters there were windows everywhere.

"I promise, we'll make it a smooth ride," Ben said. "You won't even realize we're in the air. The weather is perfect, not too windy or cold. And we'll be up for maybe forty-five minutes max. Come on."

She squeezed him hard. "Okay." He was so happy and she didn't want to be the buzzkill.

That's when she realized she'd do anything for him just to see that smile.

The thought scared her. It was a slippery slope if she wasn't careful. She refused to be like her mom sometimes, giving in to her dad's whims. But Ben had done so much for her, she wouldn't let him down.

Not tonight. Relationships were about compromises.

And she refused to be ruled by fear.

"It'll be a blast." She didn't think she sounded very convincing.

He gave her another one of those smiles. Mmm-hmm, she'd do just about anything to make him happy. And that might be scarier than the promise of any helicopter ride.

AINSLEY WAS NERVOUS. That much was obvious. He hadn't realized just how bad her fear of heights was. As they ascended, she squeezed her hands so tight, her knuckles were white.

He was beginning to wonder if maybe they should have eaten after their little excursion.

"I swear, it will be the smoothest ride you've ever had," he said over the headset.

Her eyes were clamped shut, but she nodded. *Dang.* He'd hoped this would be enjoyable for her.

"Woo-hoo. This is bloody brilliant," Bebe said from the backseat. The Brit and Jake had been giving each other a hard time, but their bluster was all an act. They were getting along great.

"Any time you want to go back, just say the word," he told Ainsley. "I can get my hours in tomorrow."

"No." She coughed and then cleared her throat. "It's fine. Really."

He grinned. "Might be easier for you to see the lights if you open your eyes." He held the copter low over the gulf so she could see the lights all across town. He'd never seen anything like it.

He watched as she peeked with one eye open and then the other.

"Oh," she said. "That's cool. I mean the rotor blade thingies are kind of loud, but it doesn't even feel like we're moving."

He laughed. "I'm holding us steady right now, but I've been taking it slow, and at this altitude with no wind, no issues."

She glanced out at the scene ahead. "It's so-o-oo pretty. I'm glad you made me come."

"So what happened to make you afraid of flying? I know you've traveled the world. You're maybe the only person who's been to more places than I have."

"Travel was my means of escape. I spent a lot of time with my professor grandmother, studying different cultures during her summers off from college.

"The last time I took a helicopter ride was in Hawaii three summers ago. When we went over one of the volcanos, something happened. We dipped down low and just when I thought we would crash, the pilot pulled the helicopter back up. But I was pretty green by then, and that pilot was lucky I didn't puke on his shoes."

"You don't have to worry about that with this one," Jake said, pointing at Ben. "He's one of our best pilots, and if we were going to crash you're in the safest hands possible."

Ainsley's hands balled into fists again.

"No crashing tonight," Ben promised. "No wind

shears, which is probably what happened in Hawaii."
He shot a glare to Jake.

His friend shrugged and mouthed, *I'm sorry, man.*

"We won't have any air currents or volcanos to
worry about," Ben assured her. "We're good. Ainsley, you know I won't steer you wrong." He meant
those words on all levels, though he wasn't sure if she
was hearing anything at the moment. She still seemed
panic-stricken.

"You can let go of your hands, Ains, and maybe
breathe a little before you pass out."

"I feel so dumb," she said. "People do this all the
time."

"Not really," he told her. "It's a different kind of flying experience. And it takes a bit of getting used to.
You should see some of the grunts on their first flights.
Nervous as all get out. But the more you do it, the easier it gets. At least that's how it is most of the time."

"Thanks for being so patient," she said.

He caught her watching his hands work the con-
trols, so he explained what he was doing. Her shoulders dropped and her breathing was finally normal.

He inched the bird forward, slowing as they flew
over the beach houses and into town. He circled downtown and then took them back to the base.

As he was landing, a big smile lit up her face. "That
was way better than the last time," she said. "I might
want to do that again. And I'm so proud of you. You've
been doing this a long time, sure, but it's one thing to
know what someone does, and it's quite another to actually see it in action. And then I was thinking, wow,

you do this under fire, with unbelievable stress because it's life and death. You're incredible."

He laughed. "I don't know about that. I've had a lot of good training, and the team I'm a part of is second to none." Once he landed the copter, he jumped out and went around to open the door so the others could exit. He helped Ainsley and Bebe. Jake could handle himself.

"Did you like it, Bebe?" When they'd been up in the air and he'd glanced back to ask Jake a question, he noticed his friend's hand on top of hers. He wondered what that was about. Hopefully, Jake was just keeping her calm, though Bebe didn't seem to have a problem flying. The last thing he wanted was his best friend upsetting Ainsley's business partner and closest friend. Jake was a "love 'em and leave 'em" kind of guy.

Then again, that's the way Ben would have described himself until a few weeks ago. It was weird having someone he felt so connected to, who'd been there for him. Made him nervous in a way, as if he had something to lose. Strange how it was so hard to even think about what his life had been like before he'd met Ainsley.

He wasn't even sure if he could do more, meaning, formalize their relationship. Although he'd sort of been watching Brody for that. What his friend and Mari had was about as strong as it came. Pretty much looked like they put each other first. That was the trick. His job, which was still important to him, had always been the focus of his life. But now, he could see how maybe it would be possible to put someone else ahead of all that.

After checking on a couple of maintenance issues, and making sure the paperwork was in order, he headed out to the truck, where his friends had said they would wait for him.

As he neared, Ainsley was watching him from inside the cab. There was a smile on her face, but something else in her eyes, something he couldn't quite define.

He stepped up into the truck. He was about to turn on the ignition when she reached for his hand. Leaning across the console, he kissed her. They were lost in each other for a good two minutes, before something niggled in the back of his brain.

They had an audience. He reluctantly pulled away, surprised neither Bebe nor Jake had said anything.

He glanced over his shoulder, and that's when he noticed that Jake and Bebe weren't there.

"Hey, where did they go?"

Ainsley grinned and shook her head. "You just now noticed?"

"My eyes were on you, babe."

"Good answer, Marine. Jake said he had one of his motorcycles here and asked if she wanted to go for a ride. It's some kind of British one and she was all excited about it. Also, I think she might be a little sweet on Jake. He's not hard to look at."

They were passing the guardhouse, and Ben stepped on the brake. "You think Jake's hot?" He wasn't sure how he felt about that.

"Settle down. No one is as hot as you. But Bebe was doing her thing."

"What thing is that?"

"She gave him a hard time, and then she got quiet. That means she might like him. Though, with her, it's hard to tell sometimes. She can be a real ballbuster, but she's also one of the kindest human beings I know. I've never had a better friend. And she's like you in the sense that she's not dazzled by the fact that my family has money."

Ben turned the truck onto the main road leading to the highway. "I'm not sure I should say this, but Jake's not really, uh, boyfriend material."

She laughed. "Way to throw your friend under a bus. Listen, she's not looking for Mr. Right. She just wants Mr. Right Now. She's not the settling-down type, either. But she usually goes for supersmart nerdy guys."

Ben shrugged. "Well, he might be pretty, but he's not stupid. Jake actually designs a lot of the drills and almost every component of the combat exercises."

"Hmm. You wouldn't get that from a conversation with him." She slapped her hand over her mouth. "Wow. I'm so sorry. I didn't mean that the way it came out. He just doesn't seem to take life too seriously. He's always making jokes and teasing."

She was right. Jake wasn't one to brag about how bright or capable he was, unless it was with the team and they were offering some kind of challenge.

"Promise me if something happens between them, it won't affect us."

They were pulling up in front of her house. The Christmas lights were on and he was pretty proud of himself.

"It won't," she said. "Bebe's a big girl and after what happened with Jake last week, I'd think he'd be a little gun-shy when it comes to women."

"Ains, you can't keep a good Marine down. And Jake's a great Marine. Might have been good for him to get taken down a peg or two. I'm not sure I've ever heard of a woman turning him down."

"You coming inside?" She gave him a shy smile.

"You've had a long workday. Are you sure you aren't too tired?"

She pursed her lips as if she was thinking. "I was earlier, but after watching you fly… I could use a little extracurricular activity."

"Like volleyball? Or maybe badminton?"

"Um. No. Not what I had in mind," she said.

"How about football? Or maybe you want to play Monopoly?"

He could do this all night.

"Not even close. But if you come in—" she winked "—I'll show you some really fun things to play with, or some really fun plays. Your choice."

He couldn't help but laugh. "Done."

AINSLEY WAS FALLING HARD, and it frightened her. She watched him sleep, his arm around her waist as if he needed that connection. Had to be touching her when they slept. She loved it.

Things were so easy with Ben. And the sex, well,

she'd never experienced anything like it. Once again, it felt like every time they were together they moved up the level of intensity.

The old saying that passion burns out fast worried her. But even scarier was the idea that it might burn out for him long before it did for her. Everything was moving too fast.

*How can I feel this way about a guy I met just a week ago?*

Didn't matter how. It had happened. Bebe's mentioning the word *love* freaked her out in so many ways. But was this what love was? Being so caught up in someone that it hurt when they were away?

The thing was, he seemed to be just as into her as she was into him. He was beyond generous...and kind...and...

He was too good to be true was what he was. They'd even talked about their pasts. He said he didn't date a girl more than once, maybe twice. What was that about? And what was it about her that made him stick around?

It wasn't as if she didn't believe in herself. She did. But he was Adonis material. So rugged...so hot.

When he'd mentioned that he usually didn't make it past the first date with someone, she'd wanted to ask him about their relationship. She wasn't needy, but maybe she could use some kind of assurance, and, in a way, he'd given it to her the night of the CO's party. They were exclusive.

For now.

And the fact was, they were good together. Living in the moment. That was important.

"What's making you frown?" Ben's voice was deep and husky. He reached out and cupped the side of her face, and she kissed his palm.

No way would she tell him the truth. "Not frowning, just thinking about all the things I need to do tomorrow."

He rubbed his thumb across her lips and she sucked it.

"You're making me think about all the things I want to do to you," he said, before his lips replaced his thumb. Their tongues tangled.

*Yes, this.* She melded into him, their bodies already comfortable with one another.

This was all she needed. All her worries disappeared as his hands slid down her body, caressed her hips, her thighs and then slid between her legs.

She was more than ready for him. Even before he found the tiny nub and used the right amount of pressure, waves of pleasure overwhelmed her. Her body reveled in each new sensation. She arched, panting, moving as he brought her to the edge again.

Then there was the tear of a wrapper, and he was settling her on top of him, guiding her down his length, his powerful hands on her hips.

Bending back, she put her hands on his thighs and rocked up and down his shaft, setting the pace, loving every thrust.

He tugged her forward, toward him. "I want to see your face," he said. "Come with me."

He pumped deep within her, the motion hitting that same sweet spot he'd found, and her body tightened before trembling with orgasm.

"Ainsley, only Ainsley," he groaned, as he pulsed inside of her.

Yes. She was most definitely his.

# *11*

EARLY THE NEXT MORNING, Ben met Jake at the airfield. They were getting in their flight hours before the big training exercises next week. The grunts would have their final exams and then graduate from the program—at least, those who passed would. But his friend Brody was pretty good at making sure everyone did well on the course.

He'd become a different guy after meeting Mari. Calmer, and more centered in a way he hadn't been before. And definitely friendlier. Before Mari, Brody had been a real hard-ass and few people could tolerate being in a room with him. But she'd brought out a hugely positive side to his character and personality.

Ben understood that. In a way, even though he was busier than ever, he felt more centered with Ainsley around. He looked forward to their time together, and in the mornings, waking up with her wrapped around him. It was good, so much so it was hard to think about anything but Ainsley.

Yet why was she hanging with him? He just didn't get it. After their discussion the other night, he'd done more research. He felt like a fraud checking up on her family, but she'd made such a big deal of how she wasn't like them at times, he had to know more.

Turned out "filthy rich" was a real thing. Her dad had started with nothing, and now he was one of the top fifty wealthiest men in the world. *The world.* From a business point of view, he had his hands in everything.

There had been pictures of Ainsley at debutante balls, and in tabloids on beaches in tropical locations. She was pretty in her teens, but she'd grown into a beauty. It was interesting that in all the pictures where there had been guys, even if she'd been linked to them in the copy, she stood apart. No kissing or even hugging.

It was weird that she had all of that and yet she seemed so unaffected by it. Not seemed—she was. They had a lot in common, from a strong work ethic, to believing in making the world a better place by giving back. She maybe did it on a slightly grander scale, but they did share that.

And being with her was easy. Never in his life had he found someone he could talk to about anything, but Ainsley fit the bill. They'd discussed…everything. From future plans for their careers, to favorite cartoons to family pets.

He grinned at that. She had definite opinions about cats versus dogs.

And then there was the sex. Heck if he'd ever had better than the night before. When he woke up, he'd watched her for a few minutes. Her teeth had worried her lip like she did when she was nervous about something. He had a feeling she was thinking about their relationship. Knew it in his gut, and as a Marine, trusting his gut was important.

He couldn't find the right words to tell her, so he had to show her how he felt. When their eyes had met as she orgasmed, and then her heat squeezed him tight, never in his life had he felt so strongly, so passionately for a woman. One woman, and only one.

He'd meant the words he'd said. *Only Ainsley.* He couldn't imagine feeling that way, whatever way that was, about another woman.

They were good. No, they were great. No idea what might happen in the future, but he was along for however long the ride lasted. He knew she was, too.

"Dude?" Fingers snapped in front of his face. "Earth to Ben. You in there?"

He'd been standing next to his truck in a daze. Thinking about Ainsley. He did that way too much lately.

"It's the same training maneuvers we've been doing for weeks," Jake said. "Are you nervous? You've got this, bro. What am I saying, you taught the rest of us how to do most of the maneuvers. Even came up with the fight roll. The Navy scrubs are still talking about that piece of awesomeness. No one is as good as you when it comes to this stuff."

"Had no idea I had a one-man fan club," he joked. "Nah. I appreciate your faith in me, but I wasn't thinking about that." The words slipped out before he realized what he was saying. Jake was smart, and there would be no getting around his admission.

"So, is it Ainsley?" And there it was. "That was a pretty serious look, dude. You guys seemed fine last night. Once you got her over the initial shock of flying, she was fine. Was she mad about me taking Bebe? It was the Brit's idea. Kind of. I told her about the bike. She said she loved them, so yeah."

The last thing he wanted to talk to Jake about was his love life. "Things are good, thanks. So what happened with you and the Brit last night?"

Jake frowned. "I drove her home on the bike. End of story."

"Huh?"

"What?" Jake asked. "I guess she wasn't feeling it. Didn't invite me inside. We talked for a little bit, and then she said 'Toodles,' or whatever it was, and that was it. The end. The whole night I'd been getting a different vibe, but maybe she changed her mind."

"Got no idea. She's a sweetheart, though. Very protective of Ainsley," Ben said, which was true.

"Yeah. A looker, as well. Kind of crazy with the pink-striped hair and the tattoos, but beautiful."

So he thought she was pretty. It was odd that Jake didn't get that far with her, especially since Ainsley had said Bebe might be into Jake. Ainsley seemed to be intuitive when it came to people. It was one of the reasons she was so good at her job.

But Ben wasn't sure what to think. Most days he just felt lucky to be able to make Ainsley happy.

And he liked doing that—making her happy. Except for his mom and sister, he'd never been so preoccupied with taking care of someone. Well, not taking care of, just wanting her to have what she needed. She'd get mad if she heard him say that she needed taking care of.

"Man, you really do have it bad," Jake said, waving his hands.

Jake would never let this go. He'd zoned out again.

"What are you talking about?"

"You're in love with her, aren't you?"

Ben coughed. "I don't know what you're talking about. We're just having fun. Like you said, end of story. Besides, what would I even know about that? Love. We're both married to our jobs, you know how it is."

"Right," Jake said. "Well, I'd like to stay alive if you don't mind. Today isn't the joyride we had last night. So, head in the game, Marine."

*Head in the game.*

Focus was important today.

And he absolutely was not in love with Ainsley. They'd only met a week ago. Besides, he didn't do love. Wasn't even sure if he knew what it was.

Yep. That was his story and he was sticking to it.

AINSLEY STEPPED OUT of her car and that's when she looked down.

"Shoot." She had two different shoes on. This had to stop. Business was booming and her head was in the clouds constantly thinking about Ben.

The man was so handsome and wonderful. And his body, he…

*Focus! You have two different shoes on and you have to meet one of your top clients in four*—she glanced at her watch—*make that two minutes.*

She only had one option. She pulled her yoga toe slippers out of her workout bag.

Whatever.

They were bright green, but at least they matched. Better than having one navy Manolo and a black Louboutin.

*What was I thinking?* That was the problem, she wasn't. She'd been all dreamy-eyed and still high on her orgasmic bliss from the night before.

And now she was meeting with one of her biggest clients wearing yoga slippers.

So professional. This wasn't junior high, where she'd doodle a boy's name on her binder with hearts and flowers. She didn't have time for this crap. Didn't have time for relationships and…who was she kidding?

Ever since she'd seen Ben standing in that toy aisle, she'd been a goner.

*Great. Just great.*

She quickly loaded up the dolly with the boxes of presents wrapped over the weekend. Normally, Bebe hired a courier service to deliver the gifts, but Craig had wanted to speak with her.

"Ha, maybe if he sees me in these completely inappropriate shoes he'll think twice about hitting on me again." With this guy, she always walked a fine line of letting him think she thought he was cute, but making it clear that she never dated clients. It was one of her most important rules. To which, he often reminded her, they *had* dated.

*Arg.*

After waving hello to the receptionist, she pushed the dolly with the presents to Craig's office. He wanted to store everything there until the company Christmas party, where he could play Santa—minus the red hat and beard—and dole out the gifts.

*Be nice.*

It was tough. They had gone out together before she started her business, and she quickly discovered that he was as bad as any of the men she'd been out with, but he was really good at hiding it.

And the only reason he wanted to be the one to give out the presents? So that he looked nice.

Because he really wasn't.

He was ruthless, and even mean, at times. There were bosses, people who liked to make themselves feel important. And then there were leaders, people who made those around them believe in themselves. If ever she was the owner of a large company like this, she would want to be the latter. To be a colleague, someone who wasn't afraid of the hard work or getting in there when things were tough.

That was one of the reasons she and Bebe kept things tight with the company. They sometimes hired extra staff, but for the most part they did everything themselves. She could always count on Bebe, and Bebe could absolutely always count on her.

Although, this might be the last holiday for that.

Even Bebe, the hardest worker Ainsley had ever met and the keeper of the budget, had said they should consider hiring at least a few part-time regular staff to help with deliveries and shopping.

But Craig. He was one of those guys who wanted to always be the most important guy in the room. She bet his employees hated him, which to her was a true judge of his character.

Yep. Definitely not her type.

Before she could get to the door, it opened and the man of the hour waved her in. "You can set those boxes in the corner," he said as she shut the door.

Any other person would have offered to help with the boxes. Not Craig. He stood there and watched as she lifted the heavy boxes off the dolly.

An image of Ben fixing her hot chocolate leaped to mind. He was always ready to lend a hand, or help out whenever she needed. He'd been such a blessing since they'd met.

"Okay, I think that's it," she said. "All of your executive gifts are there. The staff gifts will be delivered later this afternoon by the courier. Bebe checked and everything is on the truck, so you should be good."

"Great." He leaned back on his desk and crossed his legs at the ankle. He was a handsome man in an Armani suit, but his attitude made him ugly to her. He had no soul. "So I was talking to your dad the other day."

Here it comes. Why were these guys always talking to her dad? She glanced down at the dolly so he couldn't see her roll her eyes. "Um. Great. So I've got a busy day, if you'll excuse me."

"He was telling me about the family Christmas party. They didn't feel right inviting me last year, since we'd broken up the year before. But now, you know, I was hoping that wouldn't be an issue."

*Ugh.* What kind of person invited himself to a party where he wasn't wanted?

Craig.

"I'm not sure what you want me to say."

"I was hoping I could come as your date. Your father said you weren't seeing anyone."

She shrugged and pasted a smile on her face. "Sorry. Dad's wrong, and doesn't always listen. I am dating someone. I have for some time now. It's very serious, so I'm not sure what Dad was thinking when he told you that."

He cleared his throat and folded his arms across his chest. *Crud, if I lose this account because I couldn't be nice for ten minutes, Bebe is going to kill me.*

"I did mention it to my dad, but you know how he is. He's so busy he forgets. If you want to come to the party, that's fine. But I have a date, uh, thanks anyway."

"Who?" The man was just rude. He was trying to trip her up.

"Does it matter?"

He just stared at her.

"His name is Major Ben Hawthorne. He's a Marine helicopter pilot and basically the most amazing man I've ever met. We're exclusive and have been for some time." Okay, it was only since the weekend, but that was definitely some time.

"Oh." His face was scrunched up as if he was confused and her words did not compute. "I thought Marines were ground troops—since when do they fly helicopters?"

*Oh, wow. He thinks I'm lying. I hate this guy.*

"They have pilots and navigators, and also provide support for other branches of the military. You can look it up. They share services with the Naval airbase here."

"Huh."

Maybe she'd made it through that thick skull of his. "Thanks again for using our service, Craig. Let us know if you need anything else. Have a nice day." And with that, she took the empty dolly and strode out in her yoga shoes, feeling proud of herself.

So what that she was a bit too infatuated with Ben? Still, thinking about him would have to be relegated to certain times of the day. Like between the hours of eight and ten o'clock at night or something.

Her phone rang, and she pulled it out of her skirt pocket. It was her mother calling.

Not today. She just couldn't deal. Her mom and Megan had been texting since early in the morning. They wanted her to come up to San Antonio a day early before the party for some event.

But she already had plans with Ben. She'd sent them a text letting them know that she had a prior commitment. They just didn't listen.

Ever.

*Maybe I should get a new phone and I won't tell my family the number.* Never mind that this number was on all of her business cards.

She called the office.

"Thank God it's you and not your mother. She won't stop calling. I almost took her head off the last time."

Ainsley couldn't help but smile. "She's a nuisance, no argument there. Sorry, but I needed a buffer. I'm trying to avoid them until at least, I don't know, Sunday?"

"What's going on?"

Even though her friend couldn't see her, she shrugged. "Dad's trying to get me in town a day early, probably to meet more awful eligible guys. Anyway, I have plans. Told them that many times. Just help me. I don't care what you say. Make them stop."

Bebe cackled. "I bet Megan told them you were dating the Marine."

Ainsley slid into her car and slammed the door. Then she banged her head on the steering wheel. "No. Please. I've been trying to keep that news in a protective bubble. You know them. They won't mean to, but they'll destroy this. They don't like it when I'm happy. And I'm really, really happy right now."

And there it was. She was giddy almost. Couldn't wait to see him that night. That was wrong. She didn't need a man. She was a strong, smart woman.

But damn if she didn't want him.

Bebe laughed again. "Girl, you know they want what's best for you. But I admit, they can be some dysfunctional twits at times. I thought your mother liked Ben."

She sighed. "In theory. She certainly likes what he represents. Honor, duty, loyalty. Oh, yeah, and he's super-handsome. But you know how my dad is. He can be such a snob when it comes to how much someone makes. Net worth, stock portfolio...those things don't matter to me at all. But my dad just doesn't see it the same way. I was hoping to take Ben to the party and let Dad meet him. I mean, Ben's terrific. How could my dad not like him? They could even talk fishing and sports, and all that stuff."

"Kiddo, maybe that's exactly how it will be."

Ainsley gave an unladylike snort. "Right. Because my dad's so open and accepting of people. I do, I love my dad, but seriously. And you'd think my dad, since he came from nothing, would respect a guy like Ben. But he's just so…ugh. You know."

"Well, you won't know until you talk to your dad."

"I tried to at lunch the other day, but it was difficult since he brought me a date to the club. Oh, I don't know what to do. They have to stop trying to interfere in my love life."

Bebe cleared her throat. "They can't do that unless you let them."

Hmm. Wasn't that the truth?

Bebe had a point. It was time for Ainsley to set her dad straight. "You're right. I'll drop off the Wilsons' gifts and then call the house."

They hung up and she turned on the car. She breathed deeply several times and did a neck roll. As she was about to drive away, her phone dinged.

The message was from her sister.

She swiped it open to read the text.

Dad won Business Mag's Man of the Year award. Banquet Dec. 22, NYC. Private jet. Please call Mom to confirm.

That was a huge award. One of the most prestigious in the country. She was proud of her dad.

But why now? She sighed.

*Because the universe really doesn't like you.*

She didn't want to disappoint Ben by backing out of accompanying him to his CO's next event, but this was Man of the Year.

He'd understand.

Yep. Hopefully.

Then why did she feel so guilty?

## 12

BEN HUNG THE Santa suit in his closet and smiled. It had been a good afternoon. They'd given out the last of the Toys for Tots gifts at the community center. The kids had been so wide-eyed and happy, even to get the smallest gift. And it hadn't made him sad or got him thinking about when he was a kid and the fact that the holidays had felt like a time of hardship, not one of joy.

But he couldn't say that anymore.

The joy of making the kids' dreams for a fun Christmas come true had made all the shopping and running around worth it.

And it was because of those kids that he'd met Ainsley, who had done the majority of the work. He wished she'd been there. She would have enjoyed it as much as he did.

Of course, the best part was Brody, Jake and Matt dressed in elf uniforms. Chelly, Matt's wife, and Mari, Brody's wife, had both decided that Ben needed some elves to help out Santa. Elves with pointy-toed shoes and red tights and cute green outfits.

Those pictures would give Ben something to smile about for years to come. And if ever he lost another bet, he'd be happy to share said photos with the world.

He glanced at his phone, half hoping Ainsley had called. There was a part of him, a part he wasn't too proud of, that was disappointed by the fact she chose her family over him.

Dumb. He understood why she had to go. This was a huge deal for her dad. He was being honored by one of the top business magazines out there. With a big gala being held in New York, of course she had to be there.

All he had tonight was the Christmas party at the officers' club. Not quite the same level of fancy. And his brain understood why Ainsley had opted for the other event. There was no contest.

Right. Family came first.

In fact, he'd been the one to push her out the door so she could make the flight in time to meet up with the company jet.

*The company jet.* That was still a bit mind-bending to him that she came from so much wealth. But he'd never met a more adjusted, beautiful soul.

And he had to admit that it was sweet that she'd whined how much she didn't want to go, that the officers' party was really more her style. And she'd picked out the perfect sapphire dress to wear.

She even modeled it for him. And then he'd made love to her, the dress hiked up over her beautiful ass.

She'd watched him in the bathroom mirror as he took her from behind and didn't stop until her orgasm hit.

Yep, neither of them was likely to forget last night. He had another hard-on just thinking about it.

Picking his phone up, he dialed her number. It went straight to voice mail. No surprise. The plane was probably still in the air.

"Hey," he said. "I wanted to make sure you made it safe. I miss you. Just shoot me a text when you can." And then he hung up before he said something stupid, like "I love you."

Because he still wasn't sure what this connection was between them. All he knew was she'd been gone for only twelve hours and he felt as if she'd taken a part of his heart with her.

Jake's words about him having it bad were making more and more sense. But he wasn't about to admit that truth to himself or anyone else. They needed time. And they had to get through the party at her parents' house the next night. *One thing at a time.*

After his shower, he heard his phone ringing in the bedroom and ran for it, not even bothering to check to see who it was.

"Hello?"

"Hey," said Jake.

It was all he could do not to sigh. "What's up?"

"Don't sound so excited. I was wondering if you could be my DD tonight. You don't drink and you read the invite. If you have more than one drink, you have to take the shuttle service. Lame. Anyway, I'd rather you be my shuttle service. Can you pick me up?"

He wouldn't mind, except he'd been planning on exiting as early as possible. "Sure. But I'm not going to stay too long. It's already been a long day."

"You don't get to complain," Jake chuckled. "I swear if you ever show any of those photos, I will come after those you love. That's a promise."

"Don't make threats to the people you want to drive your drunk backside home. I'll leave you there with Clarissa."

His friend coughed. "No. Sorry, man."

"That's what I thought. I'll be there in about fifteen."

He was putting his dress blues on when his phone rang again. This time it was his mom. Everyone but the one person he wanted to talk to the most was calling him today.

"Hey, hon. We're so excited. I can't believe we get to see you in a couple of days."

"I'm looking forward to it," he said.

"We're making some special treats for you," his sister chimed in over the speakerphone. "Mom's been cooking for three days."

"Remember, I have that party tomorrow night. It may run late, but I promise to be there early on Christmas Eve. And I've got five days of leave." He was hoping maybe Ainsley could come up to meet them while he was in Austin.

But he hadn't had the courage to broach the subject with her yet. They'd also been busy, and with her having to leave town so fast, there hadn't been time.

"Hey, I'm getting ready for the officers' party and

I've got to pick up my friend. I'll call you guys soon. Okay?"

They hung up.

Two hours later, Ben was ready to leave the party. The party itself wasn't that bad. It was smaller than the gathering at the CO's house, with only the officers on his team. But he was missing Ainsley something fierce. Brody and Mari, Matt and Chelly were all so tight. And without Ainsley at his side, he couldn't help it, he felt left out.

As soon as he thought about her for the millionth time that night, his phone vibrated in his pocket. He stepped away from the team to take the call outside.

"Hey," he said. "Is everything okay?"

"It's so good to hear your voice," Ainsley said. "My phone died, and I'd forgot to turn it back on after it charged. Sorry I missed your call."

"Don't worry about it. How's everything going there?"

She sighed. "Okay. I'm freezing. I'm an idiot and didn't think about how cold it would be so far north. Did I bring a coat? And before you answer, that's a rhetorical question. It's in the single digits. I wish you were here to keep me warm. And sane. I've been staying away a lot and forgot what my family can be like sometimes." She laughed, but he could hear the stress in her voice.

"I'm wishing I was there to keep you warm, too. Was your flight all right? I know how much you love to fly."

"Honestly, I slept through most of it. That's the easiest way to deal with my folks. Oh, no."

"What?"

"My sister's waving me in. I'll have to—"

"Ben? Why are you out here? We're about to do the buffet dinner. My uncle was wondering where you were," Clarissa said.

He nodded and held up a finger indicating he'd be there in a minute.

"Who was that?" Ainsley asked.

"Just Clarissa."

"Is she there alone? Is she hitting on you? Oh, wow, I sound like a jealous witch. I'd say I'm sorry, but I'm not. I should be there to protect you from her."

He laughed. "Everything's cool. My head is so full of you these days, I can't think about anyone else. I don't even see other women anymore. Jake's been making fun of me. She was just telling me they're about to serve the food, which is good news. After that, I'll be able to go. Well, if I can get Jake out the door. I'm his designated driver."

"Aw, on the you can only think about me part. I'm the same way about you."

"Go ahead and do your thing, and I'll do mine. I don't want you to miss anything."

"I would feel better if you were here holding me."

"Yep. Feeling the same exact thing here," he said. "But I'll see you tomorrow night, right?"

She sighed. "That seems like forever."

He smiled. She really did miss him. "It is. But call me tonight when you get home."

"Okay. It'll be late, though."

"Wake me up. I like it when you wake me up."

"Ben?"

"Yes."

"I, uh, being away from you is harder than I thought it would be and it's only been a day."

His grin widened. "With you on that, babe. With you on that."

She laughed, and it warmed his heart. "Good. Good. I was worried it was just me. And now I sound pathetic and maybe a little lovesick."

He chuckled with her. "Again, with you on that."

"Bye," she said.

He said the same and hung up. And couldn't wipe the stupid smile off his face if he'd wanted to.

Sure, she might come from one of the wealthiest families in the world, but she was his Ainsley.

And that made him happy.

CLARISSA WAS THERE. Probably digging her nails into Ben's arm, while Ainsley sat here, listening to some of the most boring speeches ever. Her dad's award was the last of the evening. And she shouldn't have been so selfish, but she wanted to be with Ben badly.

It had caught her off guard how much she missed him. She seriously missed him, deep in her soul. And yet she'd spent most of her life trying not to get attached to men. Always keeping things light with the guys she dated.

She never knew if they liked her for her, or for her pop's money. In the end it was usually the latter. The breakup had always been easy, too, because she'd never wanted to be serious.

Until Ben.

Just hearing him on the phone settled the raw nerves she'd been experiencing all day. Her family tied her up in knots. Sad, but true. Last night with Ben had been special. That look in his eyes as he made love to her, yeah, that would be seared on her soul for a lifetime.

Maybe this was it. The real thing. The one thing she'd been avoiding until she had her career on track.

But the business was doing well, really well. Bebe had things handled with the last of the deliveries. They'd stocked up on last-minute gifts. Those calls would continue to come in through Christmas Eve. But things were great.

They'd be hiring new part-time staff after the New Year. They already had several trade shows in the works. All sides of the business were doing well.

So maybe it was time to have a life. A full and rewarding one, not just a professional one. Over the past few days she'd come to realize that she'd used her business as an excuse to separate herself from having a personal life.

That changed when she'd met Ben. He'd shown her that she could work hard and have a very rich and kind of wonderful life. And even though she spent too much time thinking of Ben, she'd managed her busiest time of year while starting a relationship with him.

She kept flip-flopping back and forth as to whether this was a good thing or not, but most of the flipping had to do with the fact that she was scared. Really scared he'd hurt her because at some point, she'd have lost herself in him and what he wanted.

It was funny. Neither of them wanted something serious. They'd just been having fun.

And yet, here they were. Well, he was there with flirty Clarissa. But she'd be back with her Ben soon.

Applause rose up around them. Her dad was walking to the stage.

"Almost done," Megan said from beside her. "My face hurts from the fake smiling."

"Mine, too," she said. Though Ainsley had been smiling for a totally different reason. Thinking about Ben.

Her dad thanked his family, who were always there for him, even when he was gone for weeks and months at a time in those early years. He talked about why, even though he had businesses all over the world, he stayed in south Texas. It was home. It was a little different than his usual spiel, and there was something earnest in his demeanor.

She was so used to her dad owning every room he walked into. He was bigger than life, bossy to a fault, but she and her sister had never doubted that he loved them. Even though he wasn't around much when they were younger, he'd made a point to be there for the important moments, from pictures for prom to swim meets. Now that she thought about it, her mom and dad had always been up in her business.

Sometimes she wished she had a family who didn't care so much. Dumb. But true.

As her dad returned to their table, everyone stood again. There were lots of pats on the back. And a little less than an hour later, they were back on the jet.

She wanted to tell her dad about Ben, maybe prepare him a little.

"I haven't seen your dad this happy in a long time," Todd, the guy her dad had brought to their lunch at the club, said as he sat down next to her.

*What is he doing here?* And what would he know about her father? This was supposed to be a family-only trip.

"Yes, he should be. That's quite the honor," she said. "I don't mean to be rude, but I didn't realize— I mean, most of the people here are family, or people I've known my whole life. I had the feeling that you and dad hadn't known each other that long."

He shrugged. "For a couple of years. We were in a meeting when he got the call, and he asked me to join him. Is that a problem?"

"No, I was just curious."

"I think he hoped maybe you and I would have a chance to talk again. You were preoccupied the day we met."

One of her eyebrows rose. She couldn't help it. "No, I was busy. And to be honest, I wasn't, and I'm still not interested. I'm dating someone."

He held up his hands as if in surrender. "I heard about the Marine. Your father is hoping it's just a phase you're going through."

**Why did they have to be on a plane right now? All**

she wanted to do was punch this jerk in the face and then run as fast as she could.

And wait? Her dad knew. That meant he couldn't know the whole truth about Ben, because she was the only one who did.

*I'm going to kill Megan.*

"Yeah. Not a phase. Serious relationship with one of the best men I've ever known. A man who is not you. If you'll excuse me, I need to speak to my dad."

She rose, but just then the pilot called for everyone to take their seats as they were about to hit turbulence. She took one as far away from Todd as she could.

By the time they landed, she was so mad she wasn't sure she could speak to her dad. It ate at her that he'd heard she was in a relationship with Ben, and was still trying to pawn men off on her.

She wouldn't confront him even though she was on edge. She didn't want to spoil his special night.

Tomorrow would be soon enough to set the record straight. If the Marine wanted her, well, she was ready to take that leap. Not into marriage. But to whatever the next step in their relationship might be.

And her family would get on board or else. She was done letting them walk all over her.

When the limo finally pulled up in front her parents' home in San Antonio, it was nearly two in the morning and she was wiped. Still, a promise was a promise.

She texted Ben as she headed upstairs. We're back. Miss you.

Call me when you get in bed, he texted back. He'd

answered quickly and she wondered if he was still out with his friends.

Ok

She washed her face and changed. Then she crawled into bed and hit the FaceTime button to call him. She wanted to see his face.

"Hey, gorgeous," he said as he yawned.

"Did I wake you up with the text?" she asked.

He nodded. "You know I'm a light sleeper, but I wanted you to wake me up, remember? So how was tonight? I bet you're exhausted."

She smiled. "It was fine. Really great for my dad. There was a lot of turbulence on the way home. You're so much better at finding me calmer weather." In more ways than one.

"You sure you're okay?"

"Yeah…I'm just really tired. I might have a tough time going to sleep without you holding me."

"Or you holding me," he said.

"Would it be really needy if I asked you to keep the phone line open so I can go to sleep looking at you?" she asked. Praying that he didn't think she was some kind of lost soul who couldn't live without him for a night.

He chuckled and then gave her one of his best smiles. The kind that sent instant heat to her core. "I was thinking the same thing."

She lifted up and positioned the phone on the pillow so that she could look straight at it when lying down.

"We're lame, right?"

"Yep. Babe, but we're lame together." They both laughed.

"So how was the officers' party?"

"Okay. The food wasn't too bad, though. And Jake didn't puke in my car, which happened a few months ago and I'm never going to let him forget it. That reminds me, I have something to show you."

A picture flashed up on the screen of Matt, Jake and Brody in elf outfits. For a full minute she laughed so hard her stomach hurt.

"That might be one of the funniest things I've ever seen. How did you get them to do that?"

He explained about his friends' wives playing a little joke on the guys. Then he switched to a picture of him in a Santa suit.

"I bet the kids went crazy," she said.

"I actually had a lot of fun."

"It wasn't too loud?" She'd been worried with the way noise bothered him that it might be tough. It was one of the many reasons she'd wanted to be there for him.

"It was at first, but then, those kids were so happy, I didn't think about the noise, or the fact that they wanted to hug me. It was just pure joy."

"I'm so mad I had to miss it. I love kids, and I would have paid big money to see you in that suit in person. Maybe you can wear it for me sometime?"

He grinned.

"What time will you be here later?" she asked.

"I needed to talk to you about that."

For a minute, she panicked. If he couldn't come, she'd have to make an excuse that she was needed for work because she could not face this party without him. Maybe that made her weak, but she needed Ben.

"O-kay," she said carefully. "What's up?" She tried to be cheerful so he wouldn't see her abject fear at the thought of being at her parents' party without a date.

"I might be an hour or so late getting there."

*Whew.*

"They had to move the graduation ceremonies to oh sixteen—I mean four p.m. We don't have that many grunts, but the ceremony is important and then there's a reception. I have an arrangement with Brody, that if we're not done by six, I sneak out and he'll cover for me. I've had to do it three times for him so he could make doctor's appointments with Mari. We've got a system."

That might actually be better. It would give her time to talk to her dad. She didn't want him to make Ben feel uncomfortable in any way. "That's fine. The good thing is we're only a short drive away."

"True. I thought about showing up tonight and waiting for you. But I can't miss that graduation and besides, it might have come across strangely. 'Hello, Mr. Garrett, I know I'm supposed to meet you tomorrow night, but I have a difficult time sleeping without your daughter. And by difficult, I mean hard.'"

Then he flashed the camera down his body to his cock, which had tented his pajama bottoms. She hissed in a breath at the sight, as warmth tingled through her to her toes. He was stunning. And she needed him.

"You should do something about that."

He laughed. "I will once we hang up."

"No, I mean now," she said. "Show me. Touch yourself—I want to watch." He brought the camera back up to his face.

"I will if you will," he said. His voice had dropped to that husky tone.

"Deal," she said.

## 13

Mostly, Ben enjoyed the graduation ceremonies. He understood the work the grunts had put in and it was a joyous time after a lot of blood, sweat and tears. But today all he could think about was Ainsley. He wanted to see her.

She'd texted him a couple of times already, and he knew she was anxious. So was he. Meeting her parents was nothing short of fear-inducing and he'd been in a lot of scary situations.

Finally, after two hours in traffic, he pulled up on what he thought was the right road.

*This can't be it.*

Ben stretched his neck out of the truck to look past the iron gate that had been left open for the line of cars pulling through. He'd thought she said the event was at her parents' home. Glancing down at his phone, he double-checked the numbers and then looked back at the address carved in the stone wall.

Yep, this was the place. As he moved farther along

the long drive and the house came into view, he blew out a long whistle.

*Home sweet hotel.*

She was rich. He'd known that in theory. But he hadn't been expecting this. The house was bigger than some makeshift bases he'd stayed at, and that was not an exaggeration.

This kind of rich was something that didn't seem to be within the realm of possibility. It was one thing to read about it and look at pictures, but quite another to have it hit you hard in the face. The collar of his dress blues grew tight around his neck. It took a lot to make his palms sweat, but they were damp against the steering wheel.

No way he'd fit in here. All those insecurities about being a kid from a modest one-parent household—and a struggling one parent at that—flooded his mind.

Her dad would see right through him.

He could text her. Tell her that his mom was upset he wasn't already in Austin, which was true. Mom had called earlier and told him that if helping a woman was so important, he should bring her home to meet his mother.

He'd promised to see what he could do, but explained that Christmas was a big deal to her family. That this party was important to her, and he wanted to be there for her.

He glanced up again and took a deep breath.

The monstrosity of a house made of stone and glass leered back at him, reminding him just how naive he could be sometimes, even after everything he'd been through.

No wonder her father was trying to find her a rich husband—somebody who would fit easily into this world, know what to expect. Ben didn't measure up.

Feeling protective toward Ainsley was something he could understand. But this—he just couldn't wrap his mind around it.

His phone buzzed. He answered without looking. "Hello."

"Where are you?" she asked. The anxiousness in her voice brought him back to earth. She was upset. "I swear if Dad introduces me to one more of his young associates I'm going to scream. Loud. I'm not saying that to make you jealous. I don't think he believes you are real. That's the only thing I can figure. I will start screaming soon, and then my mom's going to be really embarrassed and I'll probably end up on the gossip pages as they haul me out in a white coat with those funny arms. I'm…weak. I guess. I don't know. But I can't take it anymore. Tell me not to go crazy and run through the party screaming 'I have date. I have a date. I have a date.'"

The idea of her father pushing other men on her was not sitting well with Ben. Even if part of him understood why.

*That should be me.*

*No, it shouldn't.*

He would never be able to live up to her expectations. She might be okay with giving up the rich life for a little while, but he wasn't sure she'd turn her back on it for good.

"Ben, I need you." And there it was—the whole reason he was here. "Please."

"Ains, did you forget to tell me something?"

"You're wearing your dress blues, right? You look so hot in those. I'm going to have to keep my eye on you the whole time around these women. Wait, did I type the address wrong? I'm always transposing numbers. It's the one with the big iron gate."

"And even bigger house. This looks more like a museum than where someone lives."

"Whew. You're here. Thank goodness. I was so, oh, the 'forgot to tell you' part. But you knew about my dad," she said.

"Knowing and seeing are two different things."

"I'll meet you outside. We can chat. I really want this evening to be good—for both of us."

And so he promised himself that no matter how he felt, he would fake it for her.

At least for tonight.

True to her word, as he pulled up to the valet, she was there on the steps. Dressed in a dark blue gown that matched his uniform, with her hair in curls on top of her head, she looked like a princess.

She was a princess.

He handed his keys and a ten-dollar bill to the valet. "No, sir, we aren't allowed to take tips," the valet said.

"Keep it," he said. "It's not a tip. It's a 'sorry it's not a Mercedes or a Ferarri' gift."

The kid laughed. "It's the truck I want. No gift needed. And it's American-made. Oorah."

"Oorah. You're all right, kid," Ben said.

They fist-bumped, and then he climbed the steps to Ainsley, who was twisting her hands nervously. There were others coming up behind him, but she hugged him and then tugged his hand. "Come on inside, I promise we'll talk before I introduce you to everyone."

He nodded.

Inside, the foyer was a rotunda with painted ceilings and a chandelier the size of a small car. She pulled him to the left and into a private room. When she flipped on a light, he saw it was a study with a large desk.

Wrapping her arms around his neck, she gave him a quick peck on the jaw, and then rubbed away her lipstick mark with her thumb.

"You're probably mad, but to be honest I just didn't think about how the place looks. You'd asked about my house in Corpus and I kind of skirted around the fact that I'd inherited it from one of my great aunts. But I don't tell people who my parents are for a good reason. I don't want them to possibly like me because of this." She waved a hand toward the expensive-looking painting on the wall.

"I get that, but you could have given me a heads-up before I got here. I thought maybe I was in the wrong place. Yes, I figured out who your dad was, but still, I was surprised. This is— You're so normal."

"Yes. Exactly. To you, I'm normal. That's what I want. I never know who likes me for who I am. My whole life has been that way. I'm not some poor little rich girl, but I've had situations where I was friends with people because their parents told them to make nice with me for some lucrative business reason. That's this world…sometimes. But it isn't who I am."

He couldn't even imagine what that must be like, people coming after you with agendas. Never knowing if those closest to you were really folks you could trust.

One of the things he liked best about being a Marine was even though they didn't always agree or necessarily get along, his team had each other's backs. No matter what, they were there for one another. Ainsley didn't have a lot of that. At least, until she met him.

"Those guys I was telling you about? It isn't about love or even attraction. It's about mergers and acquisitions. That is not a life I choose for myself. If I ever decide to spend my life with someone, it will be for love. And it won't matter what they do or how much money either of us has."

She took his hands in hers and clasped them between their chests. "Tell me you understand."

He nodded again. "I do. It's just a lot to take in, Ains."

She gave him a nervous smile. "It is. I get that. I do. But we're good, right? What we have is real. That's what I'm holding on to tonight. The rest of this, it doesn't matter, okay? It's one night in fantasyland. And then we get to go back to our regular lives. Please, don't be mad. Please. I thought we would be driving together and I had this big plan to explain about what you were going to see. There aren't any pics of the house in the media because dad doesn't want to advertise for security reasons.

"That's partly why when they moved here, I stayed in Corpus. I just didn't want to be a part of this. I'm grateful, don't get me wrong. I've had a lot of amazing opportunities, and a good life. But I told you before, this was never me. It was just the situation I was born into."

How COULD HE blame her? It wasn't her fault her father was a billionaire several times over. She was right. He didn't exactly announce how he'd grown up when they first met. Not that it was that bad, but it was a far cry from this.

"I forgot to tell you something," he said as he drew her hands to his lips and kissed her knuckles.

"What?" she asked hesitantly.

"You're the most beautiful woman I've ever seen."

She blessed him with one of her angelic smiles and then blinked really fast as though she was trying to keep her tears at bay.

"I'm sorry I gave you a hard time. I thought I was prepared, but it was a shock. I'm good now. We're good."

"You're the most honorable, handsome man I've ever met." Then she kissed him, and he pushed away all his troubles and the fact that she was so rich.

When she backed away, they were both breathing heavy.

"You ready for this?" She cocked her head toward the study door.

He chuckled. "After that kiss, I need a second."

She laughed with him. "So I'll give you a tour. We might as well start here. This is my dad's study. He never uses it. He's got his own man cave in the back of the house with his televisions, pool table and a bar. I'll take you back there in a bit.

"It's where he does most of his business these days. Mom likes having him around, and he's never been one for sitting behind a desk. He's always moving, always doing. And, uh, I just want you to know that I talk a lot about my mom and dad but they're good people. Still, I'm not really sure what to expect. But they've loved me. They've given me an incredible life. It's just, you know, they drive me nuts. The way parents can do sometimes."

He'd been through several tours, and nearly died twice. He could do this.

*I'm a Marine.*

Funny how that statement meant so much to him. When he first started at boot camp, he'd hated it. It wasn't until his first tour when he helped save some kids from a village that was being bombed that he realized he was making a difference. And that's when he changed. The Marines became his life. A brotherhood.

A bunch of rich people were nothing. He'd faced much worse. And he was his own man.

As he and Ainsley left the study, a man with almost white hair was coming in through the front door. His skin was tanned leather, but it was the blue eyes just like Ainsley's that made him recognizable. He stared directly at Ben.

"Dad, what are you doing?" Ainsley sounded upset. Ben couldn't see her face since she was just a step in front of him.

"I was looking for you. One of the caterers said they'd seen you with someone in a uniform. I'm guessing that's you," her father said. His eyes never left Ben.

"Yes, sir. I just arrived."

Her father glanced to the study door and then back to them. "Why are you hiding in my study?"

"Dad! We weren't hiding. We were talking. I kind of forgot to tell him about...well, everything. He'd met mom, but..." She was fumbling with her words. She hardly ever did that.

"It's nice to meet you, sir." He stuck out his hand and the other man shook it. "I wasn't aware that Ainsley came from such a wealthy family. She's so accomplished and such a savvy businesswoman, I assumed what she had, she had earned."

She turned to Ben. "I did earn it," she said, an eyebrow going up.

Ben shook his head. Great first impression. *Not.* "Not what I meant. Of course you earned it. You're one of the smartest people I've ever met."

"That's better." Ainsley pretended to be perturbed, but clearly she'd liked his save.

Her father started laughing. "So this is the Marine you've been talking about?"

"No. I just invited some random Marine to our Christmas party because that's how I roll, Dad."

"Always with the snappy comeback," her father said.

"It's nice to meet you, Major. Welcome to our Christmas party."

"Thank you, sir."

"Why were you looking for me?" Ainsley asked.

Her dad frowned. "Had someone I wanted you to meet, but it can wait."

Probably another one of the rich dudes he wanted her to marry.

"Maybe you can convince my lovely daughter to give up this fool business of hers and help me run one of my companies," he said.

Ainsley stiffened in front of him. A direct attack probably wouldn't be the best course of action—especially since this was her dad.

"I'm not sure what you mean, sir. I've found her to be incredibly talented and intuitive in her business. She comes highly recommended by her clients. I was reading some of the reviews about her company after she agreed to help me, and she never has less than five stars. I've always been so impressed with her. You must be really proud."

Her father raised an eyebrow and acted like he was about to say something and then stopped himself. "Why don't you introduce the Major around to our guests?"

"That's where we were headed," she said. And pulled him away quickly. "Well, that happened," she laughed nervously. "At least he didn't catch us kissing."

"Kind of felt like he did," Ben said as she guided him to a larger room on the other side of the big rotunda.

"I know, right? I felt like I'd been caught making out in the closet with Tommy Williams."

Ben froze, and then started laughing. "Did you really?"

"Yes. He promised to teach me how to French kiss. We were thirteen. Turned out he didn't know what he was doing and he slobbered all over my face and I threw up on him. Dad heard me, and jerked open the door and I'll never forget the look on his face. He was so fierce and then he almost fell over laughing. I'd never been so mortified."

Ben laughed even harder.

"You two are having way too much fun for this particular party," her sister, Megan, said as she came up to join them.

"I was telling him about Tommy Williams."

Megan smiled. "I swear every time I see him he turns and goes the other way. She definitely made an impression that has lasted a lifetime."

"Did that happen here?"

"Oh, no. It was at the Corpus house on Ocean Drive. Haven't you taken him over there?" Megan asked. "You guys have been dating a few weeks. You should have been using that hot tub. Best view of the gulf is from there."

They had another house on Ocean Drive? Nothing there was less than a couple of million. This was nuts.

"We've both been really busy," Ainsley interjected quickly. "And mom closed up the house last time she was there. Speaking of Mom, we'd better go find her.

If she discovers that I didn't bring you right over to say hello, she'll be mad."

They left Megan and started toward another room crowded with guests. "Thank you," Ainsley said to him, "for earlier, with my dad. He just doesn't get what I do."

"Maybe you should explain it to him the way you did me the first time we met."

He always wanted to kiss her, especially now, but he didn't. This wasn't the time or place for a PDA. "I've tried. He was upset when I got a philosophy degree and then didn't go into law or apply to study for an MBA. It wasn't what he wanted."

"That's crazy. You're incredibly successful. It's his problem, not yours. You have to live your own life."

She squeezed his arm. "You truly are amazing," she said. "I know people use that word all the time but I can't figure out a better way to describe you. Seems like you always know the right things to say. And I don't care about admitting that I needed you with me tonight. I need a man who stands beside me."

That's what he had to focus on. She cared for him, and he was good for her. Didn't matter what her father thought. Well, it did. But she was her own person and could think for herself.

They could sort the rest of the mess out later.

"I feel the same about you, and have from the first moment I met you."

She smiled and the stress from the encounter with her dad seemed to have dissipated.

By the time they made it to the ballroom—yes, they

had a ballroom in their house—he'd met well over sixty people. The uniform was something different to the crowd. He could tell from the surprised looks as they passed through the room. They'd eye him up and down, glance at Ainsley and then smile.

They were polite and respectful. Many even thanked him for his service. A number of them couldn't tell what branch of the military he was from, but he was used to that.

But they couldn't hide their curiosity. Who was the guy in uniform with Ainsley, daughter of one of the richest men in the country? The question was easy to see on their faces.

He had nothing to prove to these people, but at the same time he wanted to be good enough for Ainsley.

Even though he was pretty sure he wasn't.

"There they are," her mother said, as they approached. He still couldn't believe how young Ainsley's mom looked.

"Ma'am, it's good to see you again."

"'Ma'am.' I love that. Always so polite. I was delighted when Ainsley told me she was bringing you." Her mother crooked her arm in Ben's. "So, are you having fun?"

He smiled at her. "I just arrived—" he glanced down at his watch "—but yes, I'm always happy when Ainsley is around."

"Good answer. My daughter tells me that you've been busy with charity duties, helping children and the elderly."

He looked over at Ainsley, but she shrugged and smiled.

"Yes, we've had a couple of events for Toys for Tots. My base also works with nursing homes in the area. A lot of my team members are away from home, and some of the old folks don't get a lot of visitors. So we take them gifts and visit with them."

They were surrounded by a group of women, who all said "Awwww" in unison.

"I told you he was a keeper," her mother said.

"Mom. Please."

"What?" Her mother smiled. "Strong, handsome and does good work in the community. You could do worse."

Ainsley rolled her eyes. "Ben, please forgive my mom. I'm not sure what she's up to, but we may need to have a talk about what's appropriate and what isn't."

"There's no reason to apologize," he said. "She's right. You could do worse."

Everyone laughed around them.

Her mother patted his back. "You kids have a good time. Ainsley, you should take him on a tour of the house and find him some food. Big strapping man like him needs to be fed often."

Once again, Ainsley pulled him in a different direction. "We could just hide in my room until it's over," she said.

"Now there's an idea."

"Trust me, if I could we'd be up there. My mom and dad tend to have extra radar at these events. If Megan and I try to sneak off they always find us. Like Dad with the study. It's weird. Anyway. I do want to show you the house."

He had a feeling that in a house like this, her dad probably had an app on his phone that kept in touch with everything. Oh, and he'd counted at least ten rented security types in suits with earpieces since he'd arrived.

"I'm curious about something," he said.

"What?" They were going down what was the main staircase after seeing so many bedrooms that he'd lost count.

"Why doesn't your dad have full-time security watching your house? It's all sort of hitting me, but you do need to be protected at all times. Kidnappers, anyone, could use you as a pawn. He should have an entire team following you around," Ben said seriously. The more he thought about it, the more worried he felt. She ran all over Corpus by herself. She could have been nabbed at any time.

She sighed. "My house has a security system. And when I went away to college, I don't know. The media quit following me. I was the boring one. And then when my family moved here, I stayed in Corpus. No one really cares there. It isn't a small town, but it kind of is. It's the one place I don't feel like I have to worry."

He guessed she was right, since he'd never really heard of her until they'd met. She was good at keeping her private life private. The only time he'd seen her picture in the paper had been after the bachelor auction, and she'd been with him.

They finished the tour and he bet they'd covered about thirty thousand feet.

"I saved the best for last," she said. "Well, the pool and kitchen outside are actually my favorite. But this room is a close second."

They stepped into a room that had just about every arcade game from the eighties one could imagine. *Centipede*, *Tron*—they were all there. When he was a kid he'd been invited to a couple of birthday parties that weren't much different than this. Okay, with the exception of the marble floors, massive bar with every kind of liquor and pristine machines.

"It's too much, right?" She grinned. "I love *Centipede*. Dad had to unplug it for a while when I was in the eighth grade so I'd get all my homework done. He told me it was broken. I was so gullible back then. I came in and saw him playing it one day, and I was so mad."

"Your dad plays these games?"

She nodded. "He started installing the machines in convenience stores when he was still in high school. Then he bought his own machines to go into bigger retail places like arcades and movie theaters. Then he invested that money, and well, if you looked on Google you know the rest."

"He really is a self-made man."

"Yes, which is why I don't understand why he keeps pushing these shallow, good-for-nothing twits—that's what Bebe calls them—on me."

"I'm pretty sure it's a dad thing," he said, honestly. "I haven't known you that long and I feel pretty protective of you, even though I don't have any right to.

And he is your father. He thinks he knows what's best for you."

She paused with a hand on her hip. "You feel protective of me? That's really sweet."

He put an arm around her shoulder and pulled her into him. He never tired of her scent. For of the rest of his life when he smelled vanilla, he'd think of her. "I want what's best for you, too, and I'm pretty sure that's where your dad's head is at."

"Maybe. But it's annoying the way he does it. Your way, however, is superhot." She kissed him, and he couldn't stop himself. He only stepped back when he heard voices coming down the hall. She once again wiped the lipstick from his face.

"I'm going to the ladies' room. I'll be back in a sec," she said. "Or maybe meet me in the kitchen? I could also use a snack, and I don't want to try to maneuver through the crowds at the buffet tables. And while I'm a horrible cook, my mom knows how to hire some great caterers. We always have excellent food."

"Sure. I'll meet you in the kitchen, if I can remember how to get there."

They shared a laugh. She turned to walk away, but then glanced back. "It's the second hallway on the left, go all the way to the end."

He was glad she clarified because even though he had a head for maps and directions, the house was massive.

Before he could get very far, her father rounded the corner. This time he wasn't smiling. "Is Ainsley with you?"

"No," he said. "She's—"

"Good," her father said. "Look, son. I'm sure you're a nice guy and a brave soul. What you young people do, it's admirable. But I think you know it's not going to work between the two of you."

The man was direct, he'd give him that. "Ainsley and I are friends," he said. "I'm not sure what you mean."

"I think you do," her father repeated. "You have a solid record. I had one of my staff check you out. And you do seem like a good man. But you aren't the right one for my daughter."

*Hitting him is not an option.*

Ben had never considered himself a violent man, not without provocation. But he was tempted.

High road. He had to take it. "The great thing about Ainsley is she has her feet on the ground and makes smart choices. I believe she's able to decide who she wants to be friends with, and perhaps is a better judge of character than most. You could perhaps learn a lesson or two from her, instead of trying to push her to accept any *Fortune* 500 CEO that crosses your path. You could perhaps listen to what it is she wants. You raised her to be an incredibly thoughtful and brilliant human being. You should be proud.

"To your point, if I'm good enough for your daughter, I never said I was. But she's absolutely the best thing that's ever happened to me. Now if you'll excuse me."

He had to leave before her father had a chance to

say something else, because Ben wasn't sure how much longer he could hold on to his temper.

He didn't run, but it was definitely a fast walk down the hall. Head spinning, he stopped at the entry to the busy kitchen. Caterers were going at warp speed. He didn't see Ainsley.

About to go in search of her, he heard her voice. "I told you no." She was annoyed.

"Why are you so prickly? You know your dad wants us together," some guy said.

Seriously, did the universe want him to get arrested at this party? He forced himself to stay where he was. Ainsley could handle herself.

"What my dad wants and what I do are two very different things," she said. "And I told you on the plane last night, I'm dating someone."

"Yeah, your dad said he wouldn't be around long. Come on. No way that guy is going to give you what you really need."

That was it. He couldn't take anymore.

Ainsley was shaking her head as he walked up behind the guy.

But the man shook his head right back. This guy was disrespecting her wishes.

"I don't know who you are but I promise you I've got her needs covered," Ben said. Okay, that came out wrong.

Ainsley rolled her eyes.

The guy turned around and glanced up at Ben.

"Go ahead," Ben said. "Say something."

The guy just stared at him. "It's going to take more

than some tough guy to take care of Ainsley the way she expects."

"Oh, hey, I'm standing right here. And for the record, I don't need any man. I don't need anyone to take care of me. Todd, you have to give it up because you and me are never going to happen."

"You heard her, Todd. Trust that you're not the kind of man she needs."

"And you are? She's just getting her hands dirty with you. I know what's best for her."

Ben might have growled at that point. "I'm going to suggest you leave now, Todd. And never say she doesn't know what's best. That woman is smarter, funnier, more thoughtful than most people, and she doesn't need some two-timer like you trying to make her think otherwise. That's right, I saw you twenty minutes ago with your hand up some brunette's dress. So get lost before I rearrange your face. That's what we tough guys do, ya know."

"He's serious," she said to Todd, shoving him quickly into the next room. "I suggest you leave before the tough guy throws you off the property. You and I need to talk," she said to Ben.

Fine, he had it coming. But he'd had to set the jerk straight.

Ben shook his head. Stupid. That was really stupid what he'd done. But he was frustrated, feeling so out of place. And her dad was right, he'd never fit in. He couldn't kiss up like these people. It just wasn't in his nature.

"Ainsley, I..."

She held up a hand to cut him off. "Wait until we are at the beach." *Crap.* She was really mad. He'd never before heard that edge in her voice.

He shouldn't have engaged. But he was tired of her father and Todd treating him like less than he was. He'd gotten rid of the chip on his shoulder the second day of boot camp. Yep, he came from poor, but he'd made something of himself. And he was proud.

But her father's words tore at him. Was he really not the right guy for her? And it wasn't about taking care of her. She could do that herself. True, he couldn't always be there for her. He was a career Marine. If she wanted something more permanent, and she'd hinted she did, this was never going to work.

How would she deal with him possibly being on the other side of the world? And it could happen. Maybe her dad was right, but not about the money. Everything was good for them, but they'd spent nearly every day together since they'd met. That wasn't how it would be when he was on tour. And he could be deployed at any time.

He followed her out to the pool area. There were a few people, and she pulled him off down a path that eventually led to the beach.

"I'm sorry," he said, knowing he had to apologize. "It's no excuse, but your dad said a few things to me, and then I walked up on you talking to that guy. And you'd said it was only family last night. But that guy was on the plane with you."

*Dang.* He hadn't meant to say that. What was wrong with him?

She blew out a breath and then took off her heels. "I can just imagine what my dad said. I should apologize for him. I like to think he has my best interests at heart, as you said, but I'm tired of this. All the fighting."

That was a knock.

"What do you mean?" he asked, carefully.

She tossed the shoes to the ground. "I don't need a man to protect me or take care of me. I thought we'd covered this. I can handle it, remember? If you see me as some damsel in distress, then move along. Please. I'm beginning to think you are all the same."

"You're lumping me in with those creeps you've dated?"

"No," she said. "Not really. But I'm mad. I don't need you to fight my battles. I was doing just fine with Todd."

"Right, that's why even though you told him no last night, he was in front of your face again today. You know, on the plane you said was just for family, and now he was back for more."

"Ben! I don't know why Todd of all people was a part of my dad's special night. He invited him, not me. And they're both acting like fools. My dad can push all he wants, I'm not going to change my mind because I don't care about his money. Or his protection. I'm good. Really good. All. By. Myself."

"Got it." Ben figured this was as good a time as any, even though what he was about to say tore at his gut. "You're an amazing woman, Ainsley. Beautiful and talented. You don't need anyone, especially a grunt like me."

"Wait. What?"

"It's probably best if we say our goodbyes before this goes any further." As he said the words, he wanted to call himself a liar. If they went on, it would only be tougher on the both of them. And he wasn't at all sure he could live in her world. He'd have a hard time standing by watching jerks like what's-his-face trying to make a move on her. And he'd always be wondering who her father was trying to set her up with next.

She'd been facing the water, but now she turned to him. "So, what? You're breaking up with me? The first time we actually disagree?"

*Stay strong.* This was for her. "It's not that. Just tonight showed me how different we are. I'm not the proper guy for you. What's going to happen when I'm deployed for six months or even a year? Your dad is going to keep throwing men at you. And I'm always going to wonder. Always. 'Is she being faithful?' Do you have any idea how many military come home to find their spouses, significant others with other people? We're just a mistake waiting to happen."

"No. You're serious right now?" A tear slid down her cheek.

He pretended he didn't care.

"Well, yep. It'd be best for us to cut our losses before this gets much more serious." He shrugged. "I care about you, Ainsley. I want you to be happy."

She picked up a shoe and threw it at him, but he ducked before it hit him.

"You have a dumb way of showing it, you know? A

really dumb way. Don't you think I've thought about what it might be like when you go on a mission?

"I'm not an idiot. It's scary to consider what could happen to you. Frightens me half to death. But if you're brave enough to go, then I would have to be brave enough to stay here and wait for you. I would have been.

"But you're right, Ben. You don't deserve me. That you think I would cheat on you because you were away—what kind of person does that make me? Have you met me? I should be with someone way better than a jerk who believes I'd be one of those 'out of sight, out of mind' types. I thought... Doesn't matter." There were more tears running down her face, and he felt ashamed.

He reached out for her, but she shook her head.

"Bye, Ben. You can go now. I thought I needed you. I was wrong."

Then she ran to the house and left him on the beach with a broken heart.

But it was for the best. For the both of them.

*Yeah, you keep telling yourself that.*

# 14

AINSLEY GRABBED AN open bottle of champagne before running up the back stairs to her room.

What had just happened?

Ben had broken up with her. Or she'd broken up with him? It happened so fast she wasn't sure. The whole night was a mess.

Whatever her father had said, well, he'd done a number on Ben for sure. But it didn't matter. She thought... no, she believed Ben was the kind of guy who wouldn't care what anyone else said or thought.

She slammed the door to her bedroom, and then went into the bathroom and sat on the counter. After chugging half the bottle of champagne, she burped very loud twice and took several deep breaths.

How could Ben think those things? And she'd never seen him act like...what? A jealous boyfriend?

*Rats.* That's exactly what he looked like when he walked up on her and Todd.

True. That jerk had been kind of handsy, but still.

Ben didn't have to get all protective of her. That would just give Todd more ammunition for her father.

But Ben's look of fury at Todd was burned into her brain. And how would she have felt if some woman was pawing him? And talking about getting married?

*Double rats.* She took another swig of the champagne. But Ben was the one who said she wouldn't be faithful and wait for him.

He was kind of right about the waiting, but not in the way he believed. She'd been thinking about his career aspirations. He'd told her more than once he wanted to make Colonel, and she'd done research. That meant probably a lot of moves to different bases. More tours of duty. But she had plans for that. Plans she hadn't shared with him because she didn't want to scare him off. For him to know she was thinking about their future.

Well, not anymore.

Good riddance, Ben.

The tears fell in great trails down her face.

*We couldn't even handle one fight. One fight and he's gone.*

"Whoa," Bebe said. "What's gone on here?" Her friend crossed the bathroom, took the toilet paper roll off the holder and brought it to her.

Ainsley sniffed. "When did you get here?"

"About five minutes ago. Just in time to see him storm off without even a hello. I asked him where you were and he said he had no idea. That you left him. Did you?"

"I left him on the beach, but I think he's the one who left me first." She chugged more of the bottle.

"Hey, slow down. He didn't seem like a guy who broke up with a girl. Are you sure? Because he was visibly upset."

She sat the bottle on the counter. "I don't know. Everything was out of control tonight. I think I ruined it."

Bebe eyed her up and down. "Maybe you should tell me exactly what happened."

IT WAS LATE AND Ben worried about waking up his mom and sister. There was a light coming from one of the windows of the little three-bedroom bungalow, so someone was still awake. He texted his sister.

Doodle, you awake?

She texted back. Yep.

Turn off the alarm and unlock the door. I don't want to disturb Mom.

He grabbed his duffel, and then he waited on the front porch for the door to open.

Amy, his little sister, threw her arms around him so hard, she nearly took them both to the ground. "I thought you were at some fancy party and weren't coming until tomorrow."

"Change of plans," he said, as he walked with her wrapped around him into the house. "Couldn't wait to see you guys and the party ended earlier than expected."

"Liar," his mother said from the living room.

He dropped his bag in the entry, and then peeled his sister off of him. Mom was standing up with her arms out. "That look on your face says something different. You aren't happy."

He frowned. "What? I told you earlier in the week that I couldn't wait to see you guys. I missed you." He gave her a long hug. She always smelled like roses. Home.

"I thought you were bringing your new girlfriend to meet us," she said. "Are you hiding her in the car?"

His mother was tenacious when it came to the truth. It's one of the reasons he hardly ever lied as a kid. She had a sixth sense that way, always said it was a mother's intuition. Other kids got away with stuff, he never did. Even though she had to be gone a lot between her two jobs, and then her job and school when he was older, she always seemed to know.

"She has family stuff," he said, which was true. "I told you they spend the holidays together, like us."

Mom held his face in her hands and studied him. "I'm here when you're ready to talk about it, Ben."

"Did you bring presents?" his sister asked.

"Amy!" his mother said. "Don't be rude. He's your brother and his being here is all the present we need."

He stepped back just in time to see his sister roll her eyes.

"Yeah, yeah. But did you bring any presents?"

He playfully socked her shoulder. "Yes. But technically it isn't even Christmas Eve yet, so no snooping. And you're seventeen now, haven't you grown out of the whole present thing?"

"Did you hit your head or something? You're never too old for presents." Amy clapped her hands and hopped up and down.

He'd missed this. Just being with his family. It made him stronger. His new position at the base had kept him busy, and he was trying to get his hours of flight time in on the weekends. He put an arm around both of them. Family. This was what mattered.

"I made a batch of banana bread and some cinnamon tea. And before you say something, the bread is made with whole wheat flour."

He laughed. His mom was one of the few people who normally didn't give him grief about his diet. She understood why he took care of himself.

"Sounds good."

She led the way into the kitchen, which did smell like fresh bread. He sat at the breakfast bar next to his sister and watched as his mom busied herself pulling everything together.

He'd offer to help, but he knew better. She liked to dote on him whenever he'd been away for long periods of time, said she felt guilty for all the years she'd had to work and wasn't there for him. But she was wrong. She'd always been there for him in the ways that mattered. She'd loved him, and made him a responsible human being. His shoulders dropped a few inches and he relaxed for the first time in several hours.

These were his people. It only hit harder how out of his element he'd been at the Garretts'.

"So tell us what been going on," his mother encouraged as she handed him a plate of bread and a cup of tea.

His shoulders immediately tensed again. "What about you'll be there when I'm ready to talk?" He really didn't want to discuss it. In some ways, he still hadn't wrapped his mind around the fact that he'd broken up with her, even if he did think it was for the best. The not knowing, the snap deployments—she could have it so much easier than that. Although...it meant she wouldn't be his girlfriend, let alone his wife.

And there wasn't anything he wanted more than having Ainsley as his wife. It was something he hadn't realized until he was halfway between San Antonio and Austin. It just wasn't in the cards. She might be angry with him, but he wasn't wrong about some of what he'd said. He didn't want her worrying and waiting for months at a time. It wasn't fair.

His mother crossed her arms and gave him the stare.

"Fine. We were at the big party her parents were throwing. Let's just say the Garrett house was the size of a small mountain. Not quite the Driskill in downtown Austin, but pretty darn big. But it made it clear to me that Ainsley and I come from two different worlds. Then her dad keeps throwing these rich guys at her. She was talking to one of them and I found out they'd been on a plane together the night before, when I thought it was supposed to be only family. Nothing happened between them. I know it didn't. She does not like the guy.

But it just hit me wrong. That it's never going to work. And I decided it was time for me to go. End of story."

"Did you give her a chance to tell her side of things?" His mother handed his sister a plate of bread and a cup of tea.

Amy was watching him and his mother as if they were playing a tennis match. "Shouldn't she be in bed?" he asked.

"It's Christmas holidays, and you're trying to change the subject," Mom said.

"What more was there for her and I to discuss? When I tell you these people are rich, I mean billions. Her dad is one of the wealthiest men in the country. I was helping her through the holiday season as a friend, and she was helping me.

"I thought maybe we had something, but we were both caught up in… I don't know. Obviously, I was confused because I kept thinking maybe she was the one. But after what her dad said, and then what I overheard…yeah. The guy was a jerk, but he had a point. She's not cut out for the life I have. It's done. Can we please talk about something else?"

"Wait," Doodle said. "You just decided the way it was going to be for the both of you? Did she say she felt the same? That she didn't want to be with you? I've never had a boyfriend, mainly because Mom won't let me date until I'm thirty, but maybe if you really like her, you should have fought for her? Or at least maybe not taken off so fast. Maybe she just got mad, because it sounds like you were being really dumb and mean. But she might be over it."

"You're too young to understand." He paused to take a bite of bread. "It wasn't like that." But it sort of was. "Doodle, it's more complicated than that. We… It's… I figured that I'd be more of a problem for her, than someone who was helping. Her dad made it very clear that I wasn't the sort of man he wanted for his daughter. And I'm not the kind of man who is going to make the woman he loves choose between her family and him."

"What kind of man is that?" his mom asked. Her chin jutted out, which meant he was about to get an earful. "Honest, brave, kind, loving and caring. That kind of man? Because if her father has a problem with that kind of man, I might just have to go kick his backside."

"Mom!" he and Doodle said together.

"Oh, all right, all right. But I hate to see you like this, Ben. It's clear you're not okay with how you left things tonight."

He gave a quick nod.

"Look, son. I'm not going to get involved in your romantic life. It's not my place. But when you talked about this girl, there was something in your voice I haven't heard in a long, long time. You were happy. And if someone made me that happy, well, I might think about fighting for that. Your sister makes a valid point." She gave Amy a big, wide smile.

They didn't get it. "I appreciate that. Look, it's been a long day, and I'm pretty tired."

"You know where your room is," his mom said.

He stood.

"Ben, wait." His mother rose from her chair and gripped his hand. "You're one of the most courageous men I've ever known. You have been since you were a boy. And you, as a Marine, know you never leave a man behind. I just want to make sure you aren't doing that with Ainsley, in a sense, because—and maybe this is just my interpretation—it sounds like you deserted her when she needed you the most."

It was the first time anyone had said her name, and it was a punch to the gut. Had he left her behind? No. *No.* It wasn't like that. She was better off without him. She should be with people who were like her.

It wasn't until he was in his old bedroom and had stared at the ceiling for two hours that it came to him. The tears in her eyes. The hurt that was there in her tight mouth and flushed cheeks. He didn't believe in her. It wasn't the other way around.

Not once had she ever given him an indication that she didn't believe in him. In fact, she'd done nothing but support him. Been there for him.

While he talked a good game, when push came to shove, he'd left at the first hint of trouble.

She hadn't done anything wrong.

But he'd been a first-rate jerk.

# 15

THE MORNING AFTER the party, Ainsley sat at brunch in her parents' dining room, a knot the size of Texas twisting her belly.

She'd spent most of the night crying. She didn't cry. Well, maybe at Hallmark commercials and only the mushy ones with kids or animals.

But this hurt. Ben had left her alone at a time when she'd admitted to him it was the last thing she wanted. Something had happened to set him off, before the whole Todd fiasco. It had to be what her dad had said. Whatever it was, it had changed everything. His eyes... Never in her life had she seen someone more tormented, as if she'd reached in and ripped out his heart.

And he'd been so dismissive, like leaving her wasn't that big of a deal.

But had it been an act? She had this terrible feeling that he hurt her because he was trying to protect her in some way. She kept trying to remember his words, but when she thought about him saying she would cheat on him, fresh tears came.

Bile rose in the back of her throat.

"Ainsley, are you hungover?" Her sister's question penetrated her haze. "And dang, girl, you look bad. I don't remember you drinking that much."

Conversation stopped around the table and everyone stared. There were a mixture of aunts, uncles and cousins, along with members of her immediate family. This brunch was a tradition. One she no longer wanted to be a part of.

*My heart is dead and I lost the only guy I've ever loved. Probably the only guy I'm ever going to love.*

"No," she said.

"No, you aren't hungover? Because you might have a fever or something. Your eyes are really red," Megan went on.

Leave it to her sister to poke and prod. "Let it go," she muttered under her breath. Then she shoved away from the table, crystal falling and china rattling.

"Ainsley, what is wrong with you?" her mother admonished.

"She's sick or grumpy or…something," her sister said.

"I'm none of those things. I'm…" *Heartbroken, sad and, okay, maybe a little angry.*

"Should I call Dr.—"

"I'm not sick, okay? I'm sad. I'm upset about the way Ben left last night. He didn't deserve to be treated that way, Dad." She stared at her father. "He couldn't get away fast enough. Said things I'm not sure I believe or that he believed, but…it hurts. I've never hurt like this." She stood in the middle of the dining room with tears streaming down her face.

"It's just as well he's gone, Ainsley. He's not our kind of people," her father said.

That was it. "What kind of people is that, Dad? The Todd Rightner kind? The man you secretly set me up with on Thursday night? Want to know what kind of man he is, Dad? He likes to hurt women. Only gets his kicks a certain way. Not really my thing. Pain. Yep. Not into it."

Her dad's jaw dropped. *Good.* "Oh, and Mike Anton? He's a crook. Been siphoning cash off the books for years. Wake up, Dad. You need to start reading between the lines sometimes, keep your ears open. That's right. Deal with that."

"Ainsley!"

"What, Mom? You know it's true. You know what kind of *people* Ben is, Dad? Hardworking, kind and caring. He's been looking after his family since he was twelve years old. Twelve. He puts his life in danger for his country every day. He's smart and funny and he treats me like a queen. He adores me, and wants the best for me. He believes in me. Or at least he did until he met you. And though it kills me to say this, Dad, I don't blame him. You're right, we aren't his kind of people. Brave. Wonderful, exceptional people. And that makes me sad for us."

Then she turned on her heel and left. In the grand foyer, she stood there, circling. She had to get out of the house. More than anything she wanted to talk to Ben. But maybe they needed more time. She had to sort through her feelings, and she had to be strong and sane when she faced him again. And she was really far from either of those traits right now.

After grabbing a few things from her room, she headed downstairs to find her sister on the landing.

"Not in the mood," she said.

Her sister took her keys out of her hand. "I know. I'll drive, since you're too upset. I mean brava telling off Pops, but you're a mess."

She sighed. Her sister was faster and fitter—there would be no getting the keys from her without a fight. "Fine. But do not talk to me."

"Okay. Got it. No speaking. But just so you know, I'll drive you home and Mom can send a car for me later. I'm sorry about before. I was just giving you a hard time. I thought you were hiding Ben in your room, and I couldn't help but tease in front of the parentals."

It wasn't her sister's fault her life was a wreck. "It's okay."

Her sister unlocked the car and five minutes later they were on the highway. "About the 'no talking' thing," her sister said. "Yeah. That's not going to hold up. You need to tell me what Ben said. And did you know that Bebe punched that dopey Todd last night? What was that all about?"

Bebe punched Todd. Ainsley started laughing hysterically. And then it all came out. Everything that had happened.

Megan exited the highway and then pulled into the parking lot of a Cracker Barrel. When they were kids, it was the only place they ever wanted to go when her grandma was visiting from England, much to the chagrin of their parents.

"This requires pancakes." Megan turned off the car.

"I'm not hungry."

"Yes, but I am. I skipped breakfast to drive you home."

Ainsley sighed, but followed her inside the restaurant.

Once they were inside, the smell was irresistible. They ordered pecan pancakes and hot chocolate. When they were done, her sister blew out a breath.

"So, I didn't hear the conversation, but I saw Ben alone with Dad. They were both pretty serious-looking. And then I followed Ben. I don't know exactly what he heard, but he'd been listening to you and Todd for a bit before he walked in. I thought for sure Ben was going to start yelling at him, and then you hauled Ben out to the beach, and I didn't keep following because you had that scary look on your face. By the way, I might have accidentally spilled red wine all over Todd's jacket. Right after Bebe punched him. I didn't know why she was so mad, I just figured it had something to do with you after the thing in the hallway."

"He deserves all of that and so much more. Why does Dad think he's a good choice over Ben? I can't see the logic. Money doesn't necessarily make someone a decent human being. Surely, Dad, who came from nothing, would understand that?"

Megan shrugged.

"I don't blame Ben. He must hate me. There's a good chance something he heard Todd say was what broke the camel's back. That's where all the stuff started about him believing I wouldn't wait for him while he was away." First her dad and then… It was silly, but she could see how he might think he was doing them both a favor by letting her go.

It was all a big misunderstanding.

Idiot. Well, they'd both been so ready to believe the worst.

"I have to talk to him. No wonder. It all makes sense. Why he left like that."

She rubbed her temples. "And who knows what Dad said to Ben. I'm not sure I can forgive him for this."

Her sister shrugged. "Dad loves you, and that's hard to see right now, but he means well. He just wants to make sure you're taken care of. He didn't have the kind of security we do. And, I'm the last person to take up for Dad, but he doesn't mean to hurt you. He wants you to be comfortable and settled. But he goes about it in the worst way."

Ainsley held up a hand. "Enough. Hurry up and eat. I've got to find out exactly where Ben is so I can go apologize. That is, if he'll even speak to me. What a mess."

Her phone dinged and she pulled her cell out of her bag. "It's him."

But it wasn't.

The text said This is Ben's sister, Amy. I thought you would want to know. He's at the VA Medical Center fourth floor in South Austin. Hurry.

*No. No. No.* Tears burned and ran onto her cheeks. Ben was hurt or sick.

Her sister grabbed the phone and then threw two twenties on the table. "Come on," Megan said, lifting her up by the elbow and dragging her out. "We've got to go. Now."

No longer did Ainsley care if Ben forgave her, or if he couldn't get past her crazy family.

She just wanted him to be alive and okay.

*Please, God, let him be okay. Please.*

# 16

BEN COULDN'T HELP but notice there was a loud commotion outside the door of the hospital room. People were screaming, and the noise was giving him an instant headache.

"He's here, I'll show you. See, fourth floor. The Austin VA? We're at the VA." The voice sounded so much like Ainsley's that Ben thought he might be hallucinating.

He handed the Christmas gift to the Sergeant he'd been visiting and smiled. Maybe his mind was playing tricks on him. He hadn't slept very well.

"Please," the woman wailed. She was definitely upset. He felt for the poor families who had loved ones here. It was awful being in a hospital, but especially during the holidays.

"Ma'am, if you don't calm down, I'm going to have to ask you to leave. We have to keep things quiet on this floor. You're going to upset the patients."

"Please." The woman was sobbing. It really did sound like Ainsley, but why would she be here?

"Excuse me. I'll be back in a minute," he said to the man.

Ben poked his head out of the room.

There she was at the desk, dressed in a rumpled sweater and worn-out jeans, and no makeup. He'd never seen a more beautiful woman.

He turned back to the guy he'd been talking to. "I'm awake, right? You hear her, too?"

The guy chuckled. "Maybe you should have them check you out while you're here. But yes, I hear her."

"Good. Good. That's the woman I love and she's here. Why is she here?"

The guy shrugged. "Maybe you should ask her?"

The nurse was staring at Ainsley as if she had two heads.

"I'm telling you, we don't have a patient by that name."

"Ainsley," he called out to her, his voice a coarse whisper. "What are you doing here?"

Her head snapped to the right. "Ben!" She ran to him, wrapping her arms around him and squeezing tight. He patted her back, breathing in the vanilla scent that followed her everywhere.

Then she started patting him down. And lifting his arms as if she was looking for something. "Are you okay? I got the message from your sister. I thought maybe you'd been in a wreck or something."

"What message? I'm fine."

She backed up, rubbing the tears away with the heels of her hands. "She said you were here."

"I am, I'm visiting vets. It's Christmas Eve, I told you. I always do this when I'm home. Not that I've been home much the last several years."

"But I thought…"

And then it clicked for him. She'd thought he'd been hurt.

"I'm going to kill Doodle. And now I know what happened to my phone. I couldn't find it when I left this morning. Brat has it at the house. I'm so sorry. I'm fine. I don't know why she did that. She shouldn't have made you worry."

Ainsley half coughed, half laughed. "I don't care. You're okay. I was so scared." She hiccupped. "After everything…"

He moved toward her. But she took a step back. "You left me. I mean, I ran away. But you left me before that. Those things you said…" She chewed on her bottom lip.

And he had. Abandoned her. The one thing he'd promised he'd never do.

"I understand if you don't ever want to see me again. My family, namely my dad, is going to regret whatever it was that he said to you. Believe me, he'll get an earful when I see him again. But I wanted you to know, I love you. Nothing happened with Todd. It couldn't. I love you."

She loved him. *Him.* Even after he'd been so foolish.

"I'm sorry," he said, taking a step toward her. This

time she didn't move away. "Do you think you can forgive me?"

She shook her head. "I need you to tell me the truth. What happened? Why did you say those things? You left, but I think we pieced it together. My dad, well, being himself probably was the trigger. I couldn't figure out why all of a sudden, after defending me all night, you changed so drastically."

He started to speak, but she kept talking. She did that when she was nervous. He wanted to smile, but he bit the inside of his cheek. She loved him, and this was her way of venting. Of working it out. And he'd let her.

"I told him off, by the way. Just so you know. But you didn't believe in me. And that's something." She paused and glanced left and right, as if she'd forgotten they were in public. "We have to talk about that. I do love you, Ben. Did I already say that? I know you don't think I'm strong enough to be yours—I am, though. I'm strong enough." Tears streamed down her face.

And that's why he should have stayed. Deep down, he knew she was. "I was a coward," he said. "I didn't want to believe with everything you have that you could love someone like me. I can never give you all of that, Ainsley. The mansions or fancy cars. But I love you more than life. I will spend eternity trying to show you just how much, but I'm always going to be just me."

She leaned forward and fisted her hands in his shirt. "You're so dumb, and yes, I realize that's a mean word, but I can't come up with a better one," she said, grinning. "I meant what I told you last night. I know who I am and what I'm capable of, and I can take care of myself. I know that you know that. That you respect that.

"I didn't ask you for anything. Except to be there for me when I needed you, and I will always do the same for you."

"You are the most gorgeous, intelligent, funny woman I've ever met," he said. "Every time I see you, my heart thumps hard in my chest. I have a feeling that's never going away. I can't stop thinking about you."

She beamed. "You're sounding smarter all the time, Marine."

"I deserve that. It was wrong of me to leave last night. Your dad was telling me I wasn't good enough, and then that guy said you... I knew better."

"You left me with *them*."

"We're not all bad," Megan said, as she came down the hall. "So he's alive? And wearing a Santa suit. I'm so glad I didn't miss this."

"Shhh, Megan. Ben is apologizing to me. He's telling me how much he loves me. And that he's never, ever going to leave me. Isn't that right, Ben? Well, you will have to leave to save people and tackle important missions. But you're never going to leave me here." She pointed to her heart. "Right?"

He smiled. "That's one-hundred-percent right. And for the record, I was coming to see you tonight. I'd even called in the troops to help me rappel over that wall at your parents' house. I was betting your dad wouldn't let me in the front gate. I know you don't need rescuing, but I was coming for you just the same."

"You were?"

"He was," one of the nurses said. "So this is Ainsley?"

"Yes, Mom. This is Ainsley."

"Did you apologize?" His mom was smiling.

"I'm working on it. We keep getting interrupted."

Ainsley turned toward his mother. "It's very nice to meet you, ma'am. I apologize for causing a scene. There was a bit of a mix-up, and I thought Ben had been injured."

"I heard," his mother said. "My daughter is going to be grounded for quite possibly the rest of her life. I apologize for her behavior."

Ainsley smiled, but it was a little wobbly and he realized she still wasn't quite over the hurt. He had a lot of making up to do.

"Don't be too hard on her, please," Ainsley said. "She's the one who's gotten us back together."

She turned back to Ben. "Actually, I'll be grateful forever to Amy."

*This woman is the one. How could he have let her go? Never again.*

"Ainsley, no matter what happens from here on out, I love you. Nothing is ever going to change that." He took her hands in his. "I promise."

"You don't make promises very easily," she said.

"I promise to always love you with everything that I am."

"I promise to do the same."

They stood there staring at one another, as Megan started a chant. "Kiss. Kiss. Kiss," sounded out around them.

"I know you don't like PDAs, but if you don't kiss

me, I might die," she said. "Right here. On the fourth floor of the VA hospital."

"Can't have that," he said, as he swooped in and captured her lips with his. Cheers went up, but he was lost in her.

He poured everything into the kiss, a promise of a future and of the happiness he wanted with her. And she gave it all right back to him.

"Merry Christmas," he whispered against her lips.

"Christmas with my Marine. Best present ever," she said.

"Oorah," he shouted and swung her around in his arms. But she had it wrong.

*She* was the best present ever.

# Epilogue

*One year later...*

"I DO," BEN SAID. It was done. The woman of his dreams was his. She'd just pledged a lifetime of love to him on the beach in front of their friends and family. Life was good.

No. It was great.

"You may kiss the—"

He didn't hear what the CO said after that. His lips were on his wife's. Ainsley smiled when they came up for air. "I love you," she whispered.

"I love you more," he said, and then he showed her with his kiss.

There were wolf whistles and clapping.

"Get a room, you two. Shagging comes later," Bebe, the maid of honor, said.

He lifted his head.

"I present to you the happy couple," the CO announced.

He and Ainsley began their walk down the aisle. His

mom was smiling, and Ainsley's mom and dad were clapping and crying.

After Ainsley had told him off, her father had not said another cross word about Ben and Ainsley, and he'd also given them his blessing. That was good, since they were inseparable.

Brody and Matt were his best men, with Chelly and Mari a few rows back, holding their babies. He and Ainsley weren't quite ready for that, although they had no problem practicing.

He and Ainsley made it to the flowered arbor and headed for where the reception was going to be held at her parents' Corpus house. Pictures would be done after they greeted their guests. But Ben didn't mind about the formalities. With Ainsley by his side, he was happy. So very happy.

Hours later, they were in bed at her house, preferring to wait on the honeymoon until after the holidays and her busiest season were over. "That was the best wedding ever," she said, as she turned to him and brushed her fingers along his cheek.

His body hardened at her touch. His cock was always at attention when she was around. They'd been together a year, and the passion was no less than the first time they'd made love. It had only grown stronger, as had their bond.

"I agree. And Jake's face when he caught the garter, that was priceless."

She chuckled. "I swear the CO ducked. But you're right, poor Jake. He looked a little sick there for a minute."

Ben's heart felt so full—his wife was the most beautiful woman he'd ever seen. Even tonight in the moonlight, her soft features called to him. He slid a hand down her hips and then lower.

"I love you, Ainsley. More than I ever thought possible. You're it for me. Forever and always."

She looked so pleased. "I love it when you say things like that." They both smiled. "I feel the same. And I keep wondering if this is as good as it's going to get?"

His fingers caressed her core, and she whimpered. He'd never get tired of that sound.

Her expression turned teasing and she shoved him onto his back. "But it just keeps getting better," she said, as she moved over top of him. Her heat against his cock was almost more than he could stand. He'd been wanting to make love to her for the last week. But she'd insisted they wait.

Torture.

She slipped off the long, sexy silk shirt she'd worn to bed without any bottoms. He liked her like that and she knew it. Her pert breasts, with nipples so tight, were ripe for his touch. She wiggled against his cock and he couldn't take it anymore.

He flipped her onto her back and she was giggling as he brought her ankles up to his shoulders, and then slipped inside her.

"We waited a really long time for this," he said, kissing her smooth skin. "I promise I'll make it count."

"Oh, I'll take that bet," she said, and she stroked his chest, his shoulders, his back and lower. She stared into his eyes, and it spurred him on. Faster and harder he thrust, until she was laughing, and moaning, and bucking against him, heading for the edge of control. Watching her, knowing he was giving her this pleasure—it was all he could do to hold on.

And then they were coming together, riding the wave, their bodies becoming one for those few seconds of bliss. "My Marine," she said. Her smile was soft and her eyes shone with happiness. He loved seeing her like this.

"And you're mine, gorgeous. All mine."

* * * * *

*If you missed Brody and Mari's story, check out HER SEXY MARINE VALENTINE...and Matt and Chelly's big romance in MAKE MINE A MARINE, available now from Harlequin Blaze!*

# REQUEST YOUR FREE BOOKS!
## 2 FREE NOVELS PLUS 2 FREE GIFTS!

**HARLEQUIN®**

*Blaze*

red-hot reads!

## SPECIAL EXCERPT FROM

*Veronica "Flash" Redding hates that she's in love
with her boss, Ian Asher, but that doesn't stop her from
seducing him. And together, in the bedroom, they are
creating the hottest December on record!*

*Read on for a sneak preview of*
*ONE HOT DECEMBER,*
*book three of Tiffany Reisz's sexy holiday trilogy*
*MEN AT WORK.*

"You dumped me after one night and said you couldn't
date an inferior."

"I didn't say that. I said I was your superior and
therefore could not date you. You remember that part
about me being your boss?"

"Only for two more weeks."

"What are you going to do?"

"I got a new job. A better job."

"Better? Better than here?"

She almost rolled her eyes.

"Yes, Ian, believe it or not. I would also like to have
a job where I don't weld all day and then go home and
weld some more for my other life. You can't blame me
for that."

"I don't, no. You've stuck it out here longer than
anyone thought you would."

"I had to fight tooth and nail to earn the respect of
the crew. I'm a little tired of fighting to be treated like a
human being. You can't blame me for that, either."

So, yeah, she was thrilled about the new job.

But.

But…Ian.

It wasn't just that he was good in bed. He was. She remembered all too well that he was—passionate, intense, sensual, powerful, dominating, everything she wanted in a man. The first kiss had been electric. The second intoxicating. By the third she would have sold her soul to have him inside her before morning, but he didn't ask for her soul, only every inch of her body, which she'd given him for hours. When she'd gone to bed with him that night, she'd been half in love with him. By the time she left it the next morning, she was all the way in.

Then he'd dumped her.

Six months ago. She ought to be over it by now. She wanted to be over it the day it happened but her heart wasn't nearly as tough as her reputation. The worst part of it all? Ian had been right to dump her. They'd both lost their heads after a couple drinks had loosened their tongues enough to admit they were attracted to each other. But Ian had a company to run and there were rules—good ones—that prohibited the man who signed the paychecks from sleeping with the woman who wielded the torch.

*Don't miss ONE HOT DECEMBER
by Tiffany Reisz, available December 2016 everywhere
Harlequin® Blaze® books and ebooks are sold.*

www.Harlequin.com

# Reading Has Its Rewards

## Earn **FREE BOOKS!**

Register at **Harlequin My Rewards** and submit your Harlequin purchases from wherever you shop to earn points for free books and other exclusive rewards.

Plus submit your purchases from now till May 30th for a chance to win a $500 Visa Card*.

## Visit **HarlequinMyRewards.com** today

MYR16R1

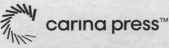

# JUST CAN'T GET ENOUGH?

Join our social communities
and talk to us online.

You will have access to the latest
news on upcoming titles and special
promotions, but most importantly,
you can talk to other fans about your
favorite Harlequin reads.

Harlequin.com/Community

 Facebook.com/HarlequinBooks

 Twitter.com/HarlequinBooks

 Pinterest.com/HarlequinBooks

# HARLEQUIN®

A *Romance* FOR EVERY MOOD™

Stay up-to-date on all your
romance-reading news with the
*Harlequin Shopping Guide,*
featuring bestselling authors, exciting new
miniseries, books to watch and more!

The newest issue will be delivered right to you
with our compliments! There are 4 each year.

Signing up is easy.

## EMAIL

ShoppingGuide@Harlequin.ca

## WRITE TO US

HARLEQUIN BOOKS
Attention: Customer Service Department
P.O. Box 9057, Buffalo, NY 14269-9057

## OR PHONE

1-800-873-8635 in the United States
1-888-343-9777 in Canada

Please allow 4-6 weeks for delivery of the first issue by mail.